ESTEBAN

ESTEBAN
LOVE'S ORDEAL
BOOK I

FISH NEALMAN

mirage

Publisher:
The Paper House
www.thepaperhousebooks.com

Printed in the United States of America

CONTENTS

If I am I because I am I,
and you are you because you are you,
then I am I and you are you.
But, if I am I because you are you,
and you are you because I am I,
then I am not I
and you are not you.

Menachem Mendel Morgensztern

PROLOGUE

He reached into his satchel and pulled out a book, one of the many volumes gifted to him many years ago. He absorbed every syllable, every word, and every punctuation mark with increasing intensity. He devoured several dozen pages and then stopped. He placed the book face down on the table beside him, and for a brief moment, clarity washed over him. If King Edward VIII of England had abdicated his throne for love, could he not justify giving up his vocation for the same reason? After all, head-of-state openings didn't come around every day, and neither did his. He thought, *It must be true that love is an unearthly force. What would Jesus say?*

He understood retirement would not absolve him of his consistory obligations; he would have to obtain permission to relinquish his duties. He stared at the wall. His chest heaved. A raging emotional tsunami threatened his breathing—and his composure.

Seeing her again had reignited the fierce passion he'd

thought long dead. A flame raged inside him like the ambient temperature inside hell. He picked up the book and read the words of De Cervantes, "Heaven has not yet wanted me to love by destiny."

And, he made up his mind.

CHAPTER 1

STEPHEN

This is the story of Esteban Ferrari.

His father, Stephen, was born the fourth of seven Ferrari children. Or was he the fifth? No doubt, such uncertainty contributed to his father's problem. Even in his early years, he became lost from being in the middle. He was twelve months younger than his next oldest sister and a little less than fourteen months older than Aurora. Stephen's father was a second-generation immigrant laborer with a raspy rhythmic twang. He'd lament whenever his son got into trouble, "That poor boy of mine, he's always been trapped between dem deyre girls."

While parts of Texas were in the throes of an economic boom, things weren't exactly flourishing for a handful of cities along the Mexican border. In particular, Webb County's poor were gathering no relief. The grassy, mesquite-covered land was as overworked as its people.

Feeding a growing family was tough, and any help was always welcome. From whence the chickens in the Ferrari's open flame cauldron came was never questioned. Should they have been stolen from S. Seen's Zahav Chicken Ranch, consuming the evidence proved convenient and straightforward. During the evening meal, Stephen usually got the parts he wanted even before his parents and especially before his older siblings. An unshared sentiment held by the family was the slight potential he might've had a hand in all this good, finger-licking food. Stranger still, the chickens always showed up in trios and quartets. The Ferraris never encountered a situation where a paltry solo chicken graced their table. No matter how large, a single chicken would never please the hungry and growing Ferrari flock.

Like many of the local parish's esoteric teachings, these fowl occurrences were another mystery. As young Stephen pointed out, "It could be that church, children, and chicken all begin with a 'ch' sound." This rationale would have made no sense to the local ranchers from whose stock the hens came. But, to the hungry Ferraris, this line of thinking made all the sense in the world.

By the time Stephen was fourteen, he no longer tolerated being called "Steve," "Stevie," or "Steve-o," or when teased, "Stephanie." He insisted everybody use his given name. His size and disposition warranted heeding the demand.

From his parents' perspective, he became a problem child soon after learning to walk, which was also when Aurora came into the world. In an instant, he transitioned from being the youngest and, by default, the most adorable to another wailing infant in diapers. Being on the end of a lack of attention is something felt more than it's noticed, and a distinct lack of focus caused him to become a problem. When he turned eight, he began to bring home chickens. But the situation did nothing more than cause a family predicament. The Ferraris were, by all measurable standards, God-loving and God-fearing Catholics.

If the chickens were stolen, that would be a sin. But to both of his parents, perpetual hunger felt like a bigger sin. So, to eat the chickens in good conscience, the Ferraris pretended the chickens arrived as if by magic. Feeling guilty, they all added five minutes to their time in the confessional on Sundays. The Ferraris became frequent visitors and were meticulous about how they chose to word their admissions to the priest. Utmost was the need to mitigate any type of manifestation toward condoning an action of theft. A family member might say, "Father, let me ask you, wouldn't it be a sin to waste the dead birds?" But other than Stephen, no one in the family knew or, for that matter, even wanted to know how the chickens came to grace their supper table. For each Ferrari, contrition was delivered in a uniform pattern that began, "Forgive me, Father, for I have sinned. I may have eaten a piece of chicken that was or was not stolen." Webb County's Laredo-based priests would seek to salvage extra details. But it was always the same, the priests were left none the wiser. None of the Ferraris, it turned out, knew or would admit to knowing anything more substantive. Since the chicken intel was gathered during confession, the priests had to settle for the fact that the Ferraris believed they were recipients of some type of divine intervention.

Whichever priest heard the confession, the outcome was always the same. Requiring penance for being hungry never felt right, but the priests were not without their ways of dealing with the situation. The priests would make arrangements to visit the Ferraris for dinner. Stephen was never put out by the extra burden the situation created. Self-taught, Stephen mastered the art of sneaking into a henhouse unnoticed—whether S. Seen's or any of the other local commercial coops. He'd round up the family's dinner, which also meant he took care of wringing the poultries' necks. Stephen accomplished this in an innate and verve-like manner. He was a young man who enjoyed his extracurricular jaunts.

Depending on how long it took him to return from a henhouse, caution always dictated events. The other Ferrari siblings would engage the priests in conversation or, if need be, stand lookout for an impending arrival. After the evening's lights were out, Stephen often used the family's old-fashioned but functioning outhouse. On his relief trips, he often visited S. Seen's, which meant the family dined on fresh eggs at breakfast. The Ferraris would consider this another day and another God-given miracle.

By his early teens, a maturing Stephen began to realize the hypocrisy of the situation and stopped going to confession; the fact that he quit cold turkey amused him. He knew everyone ate the chickens with sincere appreciation, and besides, the family's food budget provided the guacamole and other accouterments. But while his parents preached one type of behavior, they were not at odds with acting out otherwise, the pains from hunger proving to be mightier than the soul.

His mother felt ever guiltier and became fearful her son would come to no good. By all accounts, her gut was right. Besides the chickens, he'd developed a nasty habit of lying. It wasn't the odd fib here or there; it was a constant stream. He thought nothing of fabricating a tale, even when there was nothing to lie about. Lying became a type of sport, and the spectacle of the sport became a compelling reason to return to the confessional. Stephen hit upon the strategy where he could use his honed skills—the ability to lie without a second thought—to protest the hypocrisy he felt. He resumed going to confession and enjoyed hearing the audible gasps a priest expelled when he relayed tiny and intricate details of an outrageous, made-up story of sin.

One Sunday, an attending priest heard Stephen's remorse. "Forgive me, Father, for I have sinned. I told Mr. Rodriguez that his wife met with Father Joseph behind the Silver Dollar Cantina after evening Mass, and the good father had his hand up her skirt."

The following Sunday, he divulged, "Forgive me, Father, for I have sinned. I did it three times this past week with one of the visiting Sisters of Mercy." Needless to say, the priests failed to find any humor in listening to these outlandish and absurd confessions, and they were not in any way shy about doling out penance for these disgusting and disgraceful stories.

"Twenty rosaries and one dollar in the poor box."

But for the adolescent Stephen Ferrari, there was no realized meaning in this form of punishment. The penances did little more than whet his appetite to conjure up more outrageous tales for the confessional. Each week, he tried to outdo the prior week's performance. One-upping the prior confessional lie became a self-imposed test of excellence. The more contemptible he could be, the better. Lying was an art form he practiced religiously.

"Forgive me, Father, for I have sinned. I went to the Las Auras Ranch and committed an unnatural sex act with a pig." But, unlike chickens, he could never figure out how to steal pigs and still get away unnoticed.

More heavy penance. "And, put two dollars in the poor box."

"Forgive me, Father, for I have sinned. I didn't confess last month, and I still haven't said my rosaries. Oh, and I took five dollars from the poor box. And one more thing, I guess. I felt up América Ortiz. I didn't think that would be a real problem as she's not from our parish."

At the urging of his mother, his father's insistence, and continual pleadings from local priests, he left home. He entered his shared bedroom one last time. He slid a Bowie knife into a sheath already attached to his belt and stuffed a few of his cleaner clothes into a green army surplus duffle bag he'd purchased from the local Salvation Army store for ten cents. He grabbed fifty dollars from his elder brother's dresser drawer and pushed the crumpled notes into his fraying pant leg pocket. Seventeen and now emancipated, he walked out onto the street and headed toward the Greyhound bus station. In the cool morning air, he left Laredo and Webb County.

The chicken miracles immediately ceased, and the Ferraris were no longer the beneficiaries of divine intervention.

Having dropped out of school, he wandered from town to town, state to state, and country to country. North America, Central America, and South America all got to experience his freshly minted independence. He learned to barter and negotiate, and after four years of drifting, he found himself in Puerto Rico's capital, San Juan. Responding to an online ad, he found gainful full-time employment with the Seminal Import Corporation. To his surprise, he'd developed business acumen, and his superiors took note. Advancement became predictable and reoccurring. The firm decided to send him to

Mexico City to open up a source for leather goods, particularly sandals.

Stephen Ferrari entered the Mexican capital with nothing more than a letter of credit and an intense lust for the fairer sex. The letter opened many doors and aided in attracting valuable business contacts. Nothing could be done about his lust until he met Isabella. Isabella Yolo De La Vega was a perfect girl.

Standing no more than five feet, four-and-a-half inches, Isabella was virtuous, and instilled with old traditional Catholic values. She had a captivating chest, an idyllic waist-to-hip ratio, thin ankles, long pin-straight dark hair, piercing dark eyes, voluptuous lips, and a docile personality. One look at Isabella and Stephen's lust grew more pronounced. His mouth dried, his jaw dropped, and he forgot his name. Underneath her aloof exterior, she struck him as having the potential to ease his longing. But she never enticed Stephen. In fact, she showed no visual signs of interest. However, he exhibited his by sending her extravagant bouquets from *Flores de Lilas Silvestres*, located on *Hipódromo Condesa*.

Despite his working in San Juan, he hadn't bothered to learn how to converse in Spanish and had picked up a habit of drinking too much and could become crude. He hadn't seen the inside of a church for more than four years. As for Isabella, her mother taught her how to cook and how to serve a devout Catholic man, a man who would provide a pleasant home and a nice backyard. A man who would work to keep her well-attired, make boys, and attend Mass each week. In other words, he would be a devout man, a good man, and a practicing Catholic. Unfortunately, Stephen wasn't checking off any of these characteristics.

From time to time, Stephen could be focused and determined. And so, over the ensuing months, his pursuit of Isabella was relentless. He could sense victory was in sight, and his wooing pierced her resistance. He received an invitation to visit the De La Vega residence to pay his humble respects. As for Isabella, she played her part with panache. She was as demure as she was stunning. Being twenty-one, her status was that of an old maid. It did not matter in the slightest to him. He was all in.

They began to see each other with increased regularity. To help foster their relationship, she took the initiative to improve her English, while he kept insisting he didn't have an ear for language. The handful of Spanish words he'd picked up over the years could all be used in single-word sentences: *hola*, *agua*, *cerveza*, *dinero*, and *gracias*. The exceptions were his small arsenal of two-word sentences: *buenos dias* and *los cojones*. He might have developed into a fine young businessman and acquired from street smarts, but becoming a lettered man wasn't happening.

Even after the global stock market crash, he continued to find success. Mexico wanted markets, and Puerto Rico wanted access to cheaper products. Stephen was making *mucho dinero*. He lived well, worked hard, and played even harder. He lived life to the full. He performed the part of the big spender, but he got lustier with each passing day. The De La Vegas' parents saw a rich man, someone who could be a good provider, so they continued to permit their daughter to see him. As each day passed, the vibrations in his body grew. All it would take would be a few more months of unyielding and unrelenting wooing.

When it finally went down, the intimacy felt natural. He

had driven Isabella to Querétaro for a quiet meal and a bottle of tequila. He couldn't believe it! Everything was perfect, so beautiful. She was well worth the wait, but now the wait was over. For hours, the two sat motionless side by side in the front seats of his Mastretta. No matter what she said or asked, he answered in a reassuring dulcet tone, "Sure." The two of them were caught up in the moment; it was paradise by the dashboard lights.

Neither of them paid attention to the fact that she'd switched to speaking in Spanish, and Stephen had no idea what she was saying. Years later, she would blame the event on the tequila and how the moonlight struck the pink stone aqueduct.

"*Mi Stephen, ¿no ne amas?* Do you not love me?" she asked.

"Sure," he replied.

"*Mi Stephen, mi amor*, do you not worship me?"

"Sure."

"*Mi Stephen*, will you not love me forever?"

"Sure."

"*Mi Stephen, mi amor*, do you not wish me?"

"Sure."

"*Mi amor, mi Stephen*, will we not marry?"

"Sure."

"*Mi amor*, will you not take me with you always?"

"Sure."

Stephen knew he was seeing her fine-looking body close up and in person. Kissing those lips. Touching those breasts. Kissing those breasts. Parting those sugar-waxed, silky-smooth thighs. The experience was more wonderful than anything he could have anticipated. The threshold had been breached, and they would spend many more intimate moments together. But he could sense his lust waning. Excited, she told all her friends and relatives she was betrothed to Stephen. For his part, he kept silent and said nothing.

Out of the blue, he received instructions to return to San Juan at the end of the next financial quarter. Thanks to him, the office in Mexico City was now well-established, and he could expect another promotion. He made his travel plans but neglected to mention them to Isabella. Disappearing was the easiest way to break off their relationship.

Over the past several mornings, Isabella hadn't been feeling well. She'd wake up queasy and visit the toilet to throw up. She was dizzy, and she was late. Very late. Although worried, she told herself, *Mi Stephen, will look after me!* Upon seeing him at midday, her first words were, "I'm late."

"Not at all," said Stephen. "To the contrary, you're right on time. I was expecting you around noon."

Before he'd managed to finish his sentence, the light bulb went off in his head. Stephen's face turned a whiter shade of pale.

"Holy crap," he said with an eviscerated voice and a heinous giggle. He was scheduled to leave in three weeks, but now more than ever, there was no need to share his travel plans. She was taken aback and puzzled by this unanticipated reaction. Later that afternoon, she relayed the whole story to her older brother. Pedro listened and told her not to worry. He assured his sister everything would work out. Pedro didn't have to spend much time surfing the web to uncover details about Stephen. Along with his two younger brothers and two friends from the Sinaloa Splinter Gang, he paid Stephen a courtesy visit.

Pedro was the only one of the visiting quintuplets who spoke any English. In a calm but no-nonsense tone, he explained there would be no shame if the marriage were to take place soon. "The De La Vega family, the Church, and even God himself could be tolerant and understanding about the nature of young people who are madly in love."

Stephen was told he'd be welcomed into the De La Vega cartel as a brother-in-law and son-in-law. The marriage would be this coming Sunday. Stephen didn't argue and thought, *No sweat, I'll leave ahead of schedule. These idiots won't be any the wiser.*

Pedro patted his soon-to-be brother-in-law on the back and, out of nowhere, mandated, "Seminal will, of course, be asking you to stay in Mexico City. *¿Si? Bueno.*"

Caught off guard, Stephen shifted his eyes towards Pedro's and uttered the only meaningful response that came to mind, "Huh?"

So as not to leave an unnatural pause, Pedro explained the rehearsal would be on Saturday, and the archbishop would perform the ceremony, an incredible honor for the family. Unfortunately, a clank of metal fell on the terracotta floor, interrupting Pedro's speech. One of the friends from the Sinaloa Splinter Gang had become fidgety and dropped a shotgun shell he'd been twiddling. Stephen watched him pick up the shell from the corner of his eye and return it to the bandolier worn underneath his knee-length Hugo Boss winter coat. A short, mean-looking double-barreled shotgun was slung over the gentlemen's other shoulder. In another light bulb moment, Stephen came to grips with how in love he was with Pedro's sister and how, more than anything, he wanted to marry her.

"My brother," Stephen said with the broadest of smiles, "I await your escort to the rehearsal and wedding." Moving his right hand over his heart, Stephen added, "I would be humbled if you would do me the great honor of being my best man." He paused, then incorporated a two-word sentence, "*Por favor.*"

CHAPTER 2

ESTEBAN

Maybe, *it won't be too bad. It's clear she loves me.* He tried to convince himself. But, of course, his gut feeling would turn out to be correct. In the months following the wedding, neither newlywed shared a civil word. As she got closer to reaching full-term, she got bigger, and she got fatter. His resentment and apathy towards her grew, and he started to dislike the way she looked. He even had the gall to contemplate he might not even be the father. The resentment increased with each passing day, each passing hour, each passing minute, and the to-be-born child got bigger as well. Each time she looked over in his direction, all she saw was *el diablo*, the devil that got her into this wretched dilemma. *Arrgh,* she thought in frustration.

The baby came into this world on Easter Sunday. With a slight spank from the attending nurse, the baby inhaled his first breath and bellowed a harmonic cry. At that moment, all was perfect. But the moment, like many others, was fleeting. Stephen made a demand.

"We'll call him Stephen. End of story."

Isabella would have the opportunity to deal the first blow of revenge in the following years. Her husband still couldn't manage more than a few cursory words of Spanish and couldn't formulate a meaningful sentence. He continually told her how inferior she was. Stephen became aggravated by the most minor situations. In his youth in Laredo, he seldom ate steak, so his irritation caught her off guard when he couldn't get a decent ribeye. "Every meal, it's beans again or tortilla shells. Where can a man get some real food?"

When the local officials from the registrar's office came for the birth certificate, she named her baby Stephen. But she used the Spanish equivalent: Stephen, the way God meant it to be spelled. Her baby was named Esteban. Her perfect, beautiful son, Esteban. Dark-haired, dark brown eyes, light-colored skin, ten fingers, and ten toes.

For the remainder of his life, Stephen refused to forgive Isabella. As a result, Esteban grew up loved by his mother and hated by his father. Esteban Ferrari's father would not live long enough to realize his full potential. He was a conniving, lying, swindling, cheating, lazy, useless, and on occasion, likable drunk. After Isabella pulled her naming trick, Stephen couldn't even utter the word. The boy would be a good kid, and his mother was much of the reason. More than anything, she reminded her Esteban to follow in God's way.

"Jesus Christ, doesn't this kid ever get his hands dirty?" his father would splutter. "At this rate, he'll grow up to be an interior decorator, or a hairdresser, or worse!" Stephen was drunk again. "Let the kid go out and play soccer for once. How about I take him fishing?" Pausing to refill his beer mug, he spewed on. "I'll get him laid and drunk. Maybe that'll fix him up. Whaddya think?"

She chose to ignore his drunken ramblings. She felt empowered and resolute in what she was teaching her son. If she said it once, she said it a thousand times, "Ban Ban, don't grow up to be like your father."

Esteban struggled to figure out all the mixed messaging. He never knew which of his parental units was right, or wrong. All he knew for sure was his feeling of guilt. He was torn between wanting to please his angelic mother and wishing to have the swagger of his son-of-a-gun father.

His mother only spoke to him in Spanish, and his father in English. Consequently, he learned to speak Spanglish and would be completely bilingual by the time he finally decided to talk. For Esteban, if he pleased one, he angered the other. His mother made him perfect. His father made him crazy. Between the two of them, they made Esteban perfectly crazy.

One evening, Stephen came home from work and made an announcement. "We can't stay in Mexico City much longer." The comment was ignored. This was the third time he commenced the week's dinner conversation with the same comment. *How could he be thinking such nonsense,* she thought.

Setting aside home life, things had never been better from her perspective. The family and her parents had plenty to eat. When she visited her local bodega or the bigger Walmart for her monthly grocery needs, the morale of the people she interacted with was generally high. In addition, the recently elected president appeared to be upholding his campaign promises to achieve prosperity.

"The guerrillas who've been operating in Guerrero are

moving farther north. There's word they won't stop until they reach the capital. There's going to be a war. Perhaps, a civil war." Stephen paraphrased aloud as he read an English edition newspaper. He took a deep, slow breath to calm himself. He looked up at Isabella. "The government is mismanaging everything. Your brother even had dealings with someone who witnessed the corruption within the president's inner circle. We must leave Mexico while we have time, and it's still safe to move about."

Meanwhile, baby Esteban sat content in his highchair. He squished papaya through his little fingers and tried his best to stuff his mouth full of fruit. He was well-behaved and rarely cried unless he needed something. Even when he was teething, his mother would brag that he wasn't cranky. But, of course, he was; he was like any other kid. She never heard anything because she immediately comforted him. His father never heard him cry because, more often than not, he wasn't home.

Ban Ban did have one severe idiosyncrasy. He didn't talk. He understood and did as he was told, whether in Spanish by his mother, or in English by his father. Ban Ban would not speak until he was five, at which point, he not only spoke in complete sentences, but he was also able to complete a complex thought. Ban Ban could do this in any of three tongues: Spanish, English, and Spanglish.

"The guerillas will stay in the southern states. Nobody would be crazy enough to risk starting an all-out civil war. Stop it. No more crazy talk," she said.

But this was the Ferrari household, so there was lots of crazy, especially when Stephen was at home. But, in the end, Stephen persevered, and the family left Mexico City on Volaris flight 964, bound for San Antonio, Texas.

While Isabella exerted a tremendous amount of energy, yelling, screaming, and carrying on, she finally acquiesced. In the end, pressure from her parents convinced her it was her place to be with her husband. A good Catholic mother and wife must go with her spouse. Even her brothers told her to go. But it was the young rector from the Basilica of Our Lady of Guadalupe, the Ilustre Monseñor Salvador Marta Villanueva Cortés Ávila, who took full credit for cementing her decision. All those painful years ago, the rector had been in attendance at her wedding. A quick dismissive wave of this hand and, "Isabella, it's your dutiful place to be with your husband." Boom. Done and dusted. That was that, and Isabella acquiesced.

Outside the arrival gate in San Antonio, Stephen dropped to his knees and kissed the ground. "My own fair country," he said to Isabella, who looked back at him with her now standard, "You've become a real moron" look. The sun was beginning to set as the three Ferraris reached the end of their two-hour Hertz rental car ride to Laredo. Stephen was not afraid to push the car beyond the posted speed limit to hasten the trip's conclusion.

When they arrived, Isabella was appalled. To her, Laredo was a small town. No great cathedrals. No opera houses. No museums. The Republic of the Rio Grande Museum on Zaragoza Street didn't muster sufficient credentials to count. As bad as the town and their dilapidated, short-term rental house were, she thought the food was worse. Stephen tried to reunite with his family, but both he and Isabella were rejected.

A week after Ban Ban's fifth birthday, Esteban spoke his first words. It was Easter Sunday. The family had gone to church to celebrate the holiday, although Isabella felt her husband used the occasion as another reason to get drunk. Undeterred, Isabella made a large amount of food to bring to the church. She took fish tacos, beans and rice, chicken quesadillas, and pork tamales. The churchgoers, especially the priests, reveled in her culinary skills.

Father LaSpina stopped by to wish the family well. He offered a short prayer and asked for Jesus to provide the strength to hold the family together after their recent arrival. An uneasy quiet fell over the refectory as, out of the blue, Esteban spoke.

"My birthday is Easter. I'm five years old," he said. The room fell silent. Everyone believed Ban Ban was mute, but here he was, speaking up a storm.

In Spanish, Isabella told Ban Ban, "That's right. Your birthday was last Saturday. But, of course, in the year you were born, Easter Sunday was on a different day. But right now, we're talking about Jesus, and you've interrupted the priest."

"*Lo siento, Mama,*" Esteban replied. "I thought he was finished talking."

Everyone began babbling at the same time. They were all talking about how this most adorable little child hadn't spoken a word until today. And now, he had the *chutzpah* to speak two languages at once.

"Behold. We're witnessing an Easter miracle," the priest said. He clasped his hands and continued. "In Jesus' name, let us pray."

Soon after, the gathering broke up on a high note. For the moment, everyone's personal troubles were pushed aside and forgotten. The priest suggested the boy start school immediately, especially after the priest had said a Hail Mary and Ban Ban repeated it in Spanish. Next, the priest said, an Our Father, and Esteban repeated that in Spanish, as well.

"A true, true, Easter miracle," Father LaSpina said. He beamed at having his own faith reignited.

Isabella found peace over the next five years and settled into the community. Stephen was often away on extended business trips. This was all fine as she could engage with Ban Ban, which she found rewarding and sufficient. She made sure Esteban performed well in school and went to church every day. Even as a young child, he knew Saturday was the day for confession, and he faithfully followed the Catholic religion. At the age of nine, Ban Ban became an altar boy. He could say the Mass in English, Spanish, and Latin. She entertained the idea that her son should become a priest. "Such a pious boy."

Stephen threw a tizzy fit whenever he heard her mention their son entering the priesthood.

"Leave the boy alone!"

Sometimes, Stephen would offer Esteban some sound advice. "My son," he said on one such occasion, "never take sides. No matter what, don't take sides. When you pick a side, one person will love you, and the other will hate you. You'll be much better off if both sides dislike you a little for not siding. You'll find everyone will end up loving you for not taking a side." Clearing his throat, Stephen continued. "Not picking a side gives you less to remember. They might even begin to think you're smart. No man was ever thought a fool for not speaking his mind."

According to the Gregorian calendar, Easter occurred a week after Esteban's tenth birthday. Father LaSpina arrived at the Ferrari house in the evening. Stephen was away on business, so there was a calmness to the air. Father LaSpina offered a prayer for the family followed by a joyful rendition of *Happy Birthday* in Spanish, English, and Latin. Everyone was happy, and there was cake for all to eat.

"He'll make a fine priest, Isabella. I wouldn't be surprised if he became a bishop or a cardinal," Father LaSpina said as he bid the family goodnight.

Stephen came home at Christmas from being gone most of the year.

"We need to pack up. We're all going to Spain. I'm setting up an office in Madrid."

A real city! Isabella thought. *A cathedral! An opera house! The Prado; a real museum!* Not needing to conceal her joy, Isabella began getting things together.

Esteban had no difficulties settling into his new school. He could read and write in Castellano as well as or better than the other boys in his class. He even adopted the regional accent. Moreover, Ban Ban found he liked Madrid. He thought his classmates were fun to be around with all their talk of bullfights. Esteban hoped to attend a bullfight at Las Ventas, the most important bullring in Madrid. He was accepted in no time at all. The girls thought he was beautiful, as did their mothers. The boys couldn't care less, and their fathers thought he was odd. Esteban had no trouble sliding into the *Madrileños* lifestyle. As for his parents, they weren't faring quite as well; his mother found the city sunny but bleak. She didn't know anyone, and it was hard to get her customary foods. The Spaniards had a way of putting their twist on everything. At Mass, the tempo seemed off. But at least, here in Madrid, there were beautiful cathedrals. There was a great museum. These people were truly Catholic. And she felt she could relate to the prime minister, the leader of the People's Party.

"I'm staying out of the politics," was all Stephen could add.

The rift between Stephen and Isabella was as deep as ever. They could spend an entire evening glaring back at each other without saying a word or at least a nice one. Isabella would turn and say to Esteban, "Your papa thinks he knows everything. He's *estúpido*. Don't be like your papa."

One day, Isabella unleashed on Esteban. It was unusual for her to get wild with anger but this time she shouted. "Don't you ask stupid questions like your father. It's bad enough we have to live here." She stormed off into her bedroom and slammed the door. For a moment, Esteban stood bewildered, but in the proper fashion of young boys, he decided to run outside to play.

When Esteban returned, his father made an announcement. "I've decided we're going to Barcelona in the morning. The kid can listen to my talks and tell me if what is said in Spanish is the same as what they say to me in English." He turned from looking at Isabella to his son, "Would you like that?"

Esteban couldn't believe his ears. His father wanted to take him along, to have him help. He was overjoyed. Before he could answer, Isabella said in a defiant tone, "I don't want our boy involved in your business. He can't miss any school. We're not going."

Miffed, Stephen responded, "He can miss a few days. Come on, it won't hurt him. Isabella, come with me. We can travel as a family. You can miss a few days, can't you, my son?"

Before Esteban could answer, Isabella said, "Brave man,

hiding behind your son and wife. Big, brave man. He can't afford to miss school, so you can have a shield. We won't go."

"Mama," Esteban said, "I want to go. I can miss some school. Everything will be okay. Lots of kids don't come to school every day so they can help their parents. And, Mama, I'm not a little boy anymore. I'm eleven years old." He relished the idea of helping his father.

Isabella turned red. She screamed at her son. "How can you do this to me, turning on me? Siding with your father." She shot daggers at Stephen. "Look what you're doing to this boy, turning him against me!"

Stephen matched her anger. "There'll be no more discussion on this. Be ready by seven."

Once again, Esteban was treated to watching his mother stomp off to her bedroom and slam the door behind her. In the years to come, he would frequently witness this type of event. He didn't know why, but whenever this happened, he felt guilty, very guilty.

"Don't worry. We'll have a great time. You'll be a great help to your old man," Stephen said.

Yet, even with the words of encouragement, Esteban still felt guilty.

The bus for Barcelona left at 7:52 a.m. It was supposed to leave at 7:20 a.m., but the bus driver kept muttering about a malfunctioning taillight, The twenty other travelers waited for the driver to give the bus a final once-over. After a grand hiss from the release of pressurized air, the bus pulled away and gained speed.

Traffic was generally light. Just a few trucks, a steady stream of 250cc motorbikes, the usual smattering of two and four-door hatchbacks, and the odd police car. Nevertheless,

Isabella was determined to make the worst of the trip and complained at every discomfiture. Even the other passengers began to get irritated by her continual whining. And she never missed an opportunity to say to Esteban, "You're the reason I have to put up with this."

According to the schedule, the trip would cover the five-hundred-kilometers in a little over seven hours, and the driver was attempting to make up for the late start. Midway through the trip, as the bus approached Zaragoza, a police car pulled alongside and directed the driver to pull over. He was told to drive to a cantina about one kilometer up the road toward Valenzuela. Everyone was ordered off the bus and inside. This gave the passengers a chance to eat and stretch. Isabella complained and blamed the two men in her life for her hardship. Two hours later, the passengers were ordered back onto the bus. The bus was given an escort for the next several kilometers, and without any fanfare, the escort stopped. The bus continued, and because he didn't know any better, Esteban got out of his seat and walked to the front to ask the driver why they had endured a delay. The driver was surprised by the question, but seeing as it was only a little boy, he answered, "A group of terrorists tried to make some trouble. Probably, some bandits or some Basque bastards. Hey kid, go back to your parents and sit down."

The rest of the way to Barcelona was uneventful, and the bus pulled into the square at close to 5:00 p.m. Everyone was weary and tired. As was the custom, Stephen had to bribe the hotel desk clerk for a room with an en suite bathroom. Bribery was a way of life in Spain.

CHAPTER 3

SIGNORE ROMERO

The next three days flew by. Esteban listened to the many business conversations but heard no discernible differences. His father negotiated the lease of several cargo ships. One trick Stephen used was the threat of going to Valencia or Cartagena to get his ships. The Spanish captains were quick to cave in. He set up a network of moving goods to and from the Americas by way of Palermo in Sicily. The extra leg kept the dockworkers busy and helped support the active black and gray markets.

Friday morning, the Ferrari trio reboarded the bus for the return trip to Madrid. Unfortunately for Isabella, the travel was every bit as uncomfortable. Once again, the bus stopped at the same cantina in Zaragoza. This would become a regular unscheduled stop, much to the owner's delight. All kinds of bribes were transacted in Spain, and the cantina's owner obliged by stepping up to the plate. Stephen was quick to recognize and take full advantage of the situation in his own dealings.

The following month, Stephen decided the train would be easier and help cut the travel time. It was almost a pleasure. However, Isabella still found plenty to complain about and did so with gusto. The Ferraris began to make the trip once a month, and Esteban became the envy of his classmates. He was delighted in his newfound ability to help his father and gain adoration. As for Isabella, her complaining and infusing Esteban with guilt became worse and worse. Over time, his father's meetings became shorter because of a new business associate. One time, on the return trip to Madrid, Stephen said out of the blue, "That Romero, he's really something," and laughed to himself.

"What do you mean, Papa?" Esteban asked.

Stephen was startled by the question because he hadn't realized he'd spoken aloud. As far as he knew, he'd been lost in thought. He recovered his composure and said, "You see how he always has everything ready? No matter what needs to be done, he can get it sorted. He's a good man to do business with." The conversation was over, and Stephen went back to his papers.

Isabella spoke up. "He can't be trusted. He's an atheist. How can an Italian not be Catholic?" Stephen closed his eyes and shook his head. "You never listen to me." Isabella began to wail and left their private train compartment.

When the door closed, Stephen looked at Esteban and smirked. "No bedroom doors on this train!" and returned to his papers.

Isabella was wrong. Signore Romero could be trusted, and in ways, Esteban and Isabella would never learn. He never had trouble obtaining visas. He knew everyone, and who to bribe and how much. As a result, the business prospered, and Seminal continued to expand.

Signore Romero began visiting Madrid on a regular basis and would always dine with the family. He brought gifts of impeccable delicacies, which made Isabella stop resenting his intrusions. As if to show off, she cooked outstanding meals when he came. He was always polite and full of praise for her extraordinary efforts. When speaking to Esteban, he'd oscillate between Spanish and Italian. Esteban enjoyed his company because of the chance to hear and learn another language. The Signore told marvelous stories about his worldly adventures, all so romantic to the little boy.

On one of his visits, Signore Romero asked Esteban, "Do they teach you history in your school?"

"Yes," Esteban answered.

"What do they teach you about General Francisco Franco?"

"They teach us about the Spanish miracle," Esteban replied.

"Yes, yes. I can see why they would tell you that. Would you like to ask the fathers at your school some other challenging questions?" Romero asked with a mischievous grin.

Sensing the fun to be had, Esteban replied, "Yes."

"Tomorrow, be sure to ask them to tell you about the deals Franco made with the Pope for his support. They allowed Franco to kill thousands of innocent people, especially those that disagreed with him."

Esteban couldn't wait. As soon as he got his chance, he raised his hand. The father paled after hearing Esteban's question. "Who told you to ask that?"

Esteban lied for fear of getting his friend in trouble. Looking down at the floor he said, "No one."

The priest stared at Esteban and said, "A true Catholic doesn't ask questions like that." The issue was dropped.

After school, Esteban went to the chapel to say confession for his sin of lying. The confessor was his teacher, already in the confessional when Esteban entered.

"Forgive me, Father, for I have sinned. It has been four days since my last confession," Esteban said.

"What is your sin, my son."

"Today, I told a lie."

The priest wasn't paying attention. After all, this was another schoolboy confession. He said, "Say three Hail Mary's and three Our Fathers and go and sin no more."

It wasn't until after he'd left the confessional that the priest realized what had transpired. He tried to call Esteban back, but the boy was already out of hearing range and off playing soccer. It was his turn to be Messi.

That night, after dinner, the Signore said, "I have a few more questions you can ask at school." Afraid to tell Signore what happened, Esteban sat and listened.

"Ask the following," the Signore said in Italian. "What was the Spanish Inquisition, and why did it happen?"

First, he paused to make sure the boy understood the question. When satisfied, Romero continued. "What did Spain do to the indigenous Indians of the New World? And, what happened to all that gold?" The Signore paused to pat his lips with a handkerchief. Switching back to Spanish, he said, "I'll be back again next week, and you can tell me what happened."

Esteban had to build up the courage to ask his questions,

and it wasn't until Friday afternoon that he summoned the bravery to raise his hand. With a slow and deliberate meter, the words for his question came out. The priest looked like he'd been kicked in the pants. Esteban, feeling he was on a roll, spurted out his second question before the priest could attempt to address the first. The priest's eyes bulged in disbelief, and didn't answer. Instead, he demanded Esteban stay behind after school. Once again, the other kids watched wide-eyed. There wasn't a sound in the room. The end of the school day wasn't too far away, and the priest took the opportunity to pull Esteban aside. With respect, the priest inquired who was goading him to ask these questions.

Afraid, Esteban once again espoused a lie. "No one."

The priest was exasperated. He knew Esteban was lying because of what had happened previously. Because the confessional was sacred, he couldn't use the information and had to devise an alternative tack.

"Esteban, you were told to ask those questions by someone hoping to weaken your faith. Don't be fooled. The answers are not important. What's done is done, and good Catholics don't question these things. Faith is what's important. Tell your father I will stop by your house tomorrow afternoon. Now run on home."

Esteban hurried home, wondering how he would tell his parents. He was struck by the thought his father didn't speak Spanish. Esteban would have to interpret what the priest was saying. He could try and make it sound not as bad. Over dinner, he told his parents about the impending visit in an off-hand way. He managed to go out to play before the possible importance sank in. The following morning, Esteban went with his mother to church to say confession. He began the litany, not knowing who the father confessor was, and confessed his sin of lying for a second time. The same father heard his confession and, this time, paid attention.

"What was your lie, my son?" he asked.

Esteban told him the whole story of Signore Romero and the questions. The priest found himself in a precarious situation about how to punish the boy so he wouldn't lie again and not ask delicate things.

"Lying is a serious sin," the priest said. "As wrong as lying is, lying to a priest is worse. It is the same as lying to God. Your penance is to say one rosary every day for two weeks and to put your whole allowance in the poor box for the next three weeks. Perform this act of contrition. Go and sin no more."

Esteban was crushed. It would take an hour to say a whole rosary. And giving up his entire allowance for three weeks, he was too ashamed to tell his mama. So, he bore his guilt in quiet. He still had the visit to face. The priest's call was short, and he only met with Isabella as Stephen wasn't home. Nevertheless, he explained Esteban's questions and how he believed the boy had been coached. He told her not to worry about the situation as he had explained the issue and was convinced Esteban had faith and would pray for guidance. The meeting was over. Nothing was said to her son afterward. Isabella, of course, raised hell with Stephen about Signore's bad influence on their son.

The following Tuesday after dinner, the Signore said to Esteban, "Let's take a walk. I'll buy you a horchata," and they left the table before Isabella could stop them. Once they were outside, Romero said, "You look like you've lost your best friend. Tell me what happened."

Esteban told him the whole story, including the harsh

penance. The Signore listened, and when Esteban finished, he explained his point of view on the three questions.

"Franco oppressed all who opposed him. That included conservatives and non-Catholics. The Pope turned a blind eye to the war and murder because Franco promised to keep Spain Catholic no matter what happened. He kept his promise. At the time, the whole world condemned Franco, but the Pope kept quiet. It's something to think about, yes? Pope Pius the Twelfth kept quiet while Mussolini and Hitler came to power. He never once raised his voice in protest. But that's nothing new for popes. As long as they can run their Church and the Holy See, they don't seem to care who's in power." Romero was on a roll. "Spain had a great fleet of ships during the Middle Ages. She sent explorers to find new unclaimed lands. She sent the Italian, Christopher Columbus, to find a shortcut to India. The Church said it was impossible that he would fall off the world. The world was thought to be flat at the time. So, on the one hand, they were right. Columbus wouldn't find India, but he would go on to find something much better, America."

The two were next in line. "*Dos horchatas, por favor.*"

"Here," Romero said to Esteban. "Now, where were we? Ah, yes." Romero took a sip and continued. "Once Columbus discovered America, what did Spain and the Church do? They sent armies to kill and enslave the indigenous natives. They raped the women, killed the children, and stole their wealth. Tons and tons of silver and gold. Those they didn't kill, they forced into converting to Catholicism. They spread the true word of the Church. It's good, huh?" He pointed to the horchata.

"Yes, Signore."

"Good. Good. Now, those being conquered were armed with spears and knives and thought white men were gods. The natives weren't suspicious about the power of the guns and gunpowder. The looting was easy. The Spanish rulers forced everyone to become Catholic. In turn, they believed if converting was good enough for the Indians, it would be good for everyone. Peaceful Jews and Moors were convicted of heresy and tortured until they converted. They were burned at the stake if they were strong in their convictions and wouldn't convert. The lucky ones escaped with their lives and little else. Their personal belongings, all their wealth, were confiscated by the Crown and Church. All this was done in the name of God, and the Christ, and to spread the true word. Untold thousands were slain. Untold millions were slain. It's something to think about, yes? Now, would you like another?"

The barrage of information was overwhelming for Esteban. Finishing his second horchata was all he could muster, and he remained silent during the walk back. But it felt like there was something to think about. When they returned home, Esteban was ordered straight to bed and missed the argument between his parents and the Signore. Isabella wanted nothing to interfere with her boy's Catholic education. The Signore agreed not to influence him any further. Stephen was passive on the subject, although he felt there should be other things in his son's life.

Before leaving for school the next morning, Isabella said, "Don't pay any attention to what the Signore says. Believe your priests. They are men of God. They know what is best and, moreover, what is right."

Esteban thought it all over that evening and for the days

following. He thought about it while he said his rosary every day. He thought about it when he put his allowance into the poor box. He thought about it while the priests taught and preached. Finally, time passed, and he stopped thinking about it. After all, he was the one who had to live with his mother. He was the one who had to put his allowance in the poor box, and he was the one who had to say the rosary. Now, that was something to think about!

Esteban's friendship with the Signore changed, and they weren't as close as they were before the questions. Esteban went out of his way to demonstrate his faith. One lesson the experience taught Esteban was that some questions should never be asked. Except for the arguments between his parents and the frequent slamming of the bedroom door, life moved along. At the close of the school year, Stephen sat at the dinner table and made an announcement.

"Pack up. We're moving to Frankfurt. My job here is through, and the organization wants to open up in Germany. We're to be there by September."

Isabella didn't know whether to complain about having to move again or rejoice because she was leaving Spain. "When exactly?" she asked.

"As soon as possible," Stephen answered.

"But it's only June. So, what do we do over the summer?" a deflated Isabella said.

"I thought you'd like a vacation in Rome," Stephen said with a sly smile. "I've already arranged flights and living accommodations."

For the first time in years, she felt happy. Immediately after dinner, she began the process of sorting and packing. In three days, they would be ready to go. On the fourth day, they departed from the Adolfo Suárez Madrid-Barajas Airport. Signore Romero drove the family and, after parking the vehicle, walked with them to the departure lounge. He told Stephen he would see him soon. He kissed Isabella's hand and wished her well, and finally, turning to Esteban, he said, "My young man, good luck. Stay well until we meet again. Germany will give you much to think about. *Bon voyage.*"

CHAPTER 4

LUKAS

The trip lasted a little more than three hours. For once, nobody pouted, nobody complained, and nobody created an environment of hostility. Even though the Ferraris didn't hold a European passport, they were allowed to enter Italy without clearing customs, all courtesy of starting their trip from another EU country. As a devout Catholic, Isabella was excited to be in Rome and next to Vatican City.

"Are we eating out tonight?" Isabella asked.

"Yes, we're having dinner near the Pantheon. A place called, *Osteria Trattoria da Fortunata*."

The restaurant was a small family affair, and Isabella decided to take it upon herself to venture back into the kitchen. She spoke to the chef and gave him directions on a dessert she wanted him to make. The chef grumbled but complied. Later, after everyone had gone to bed, Esteban heard some strange noises coming from his parents' bedroom. He was still too young and far too innocent to know the sounds of lovemaking. The next day, Isabella couldn't believe her eyes as she entered the lobby of her accommodations. She recognized the man before her. Heavier and older, and sporting a bit of gray, it was her eldest brother, Pedro. He had donned a well-tailored suit and well-shined shoes. The greetings and kisses and questions were the same as those exchanged by long-parted families the world over. Pedro, however, had a business-like air about him. Stephen appeared moments later. He approached Pedro and shook his hand with vigor. In English, Pedro asked if they all had a good flight and if their accommodations were all acceptable.

"Yes, yes, very much so," Stephen said.

Pedro turned to Isabella and said, "Forgive me. I have work to do. I'll be by again tomorrow morning." He hugged his sister. "I have given the concierge instructions for your welfare. Anything you wish, just ask." He turned and left. Esteban was overlooked during the whole exchange.

"What was all that about?" Isabella asked. Her brother seemed to pay more attention to him than to her.

"Pedro will tell you all about it tomorrow."

"No. I want to know about it now," she said.

"Tomorrow," Stephen said. His voice emanated a particular steel that neither Isabella nor Esteban had heard before. For the moment, the subject was closed.

Dinner night had a feeling different from the prior evening.

"How long have you been working with him?" Isabella asked with a frigid tone.

"A while," Stephen answered.

"Why didn't you tell me?"

"He didn't want me to."

"Why?"

"I promise, he'll tell you tomorrow. Please, pass the bread. No more about it tonight?"

By the time everyone got back to their hotel, it was late. There was a message waiting for them from Genoa. Pedro's business dealings would keep him detained another day. When he finally arrived at the hotel, he was riding in the back of a brand-new, Mercedes S-class sedan and appeared to be a man of importance. He was dressed in a sharp charcoal gray sharkskin suit sporting a patterned pocket square with a flat fold, a white shirt, a small polka-dotted red tie, and a pair of black shoes. Everything was complemented by a nice pearl-gray fedora. Pedro ushered the Ferraris into his car and immediately tried to hush Isabella's many questions. Originally, Pedro had wanted their mother and father to join him in Italy, but unfortunately, they were caught up in an unsuccessful guerrilla attack on the outskirts of Mexico City. Isabella's and Pedro's two other brothers were still alive and chose to stay. In the following days, Isabella noticed her brother treated Stephen with respect, and Pedro's attending staff treated her brother like a king.

She asked Stephen, "How?"

He replied, "Let's save that question for another time."

Being adventuresome, Esteban sometimes wandered off alone when Isabella wasn't watching. On one of these explorations, he encountered a group of boys about his age and approached them to make friends. They were street orphans and not apt to accept an invitation. Homeless and parentless, they lived by robbery and violence. Like moths drawn to the light, they fell on him, taking his clothes and his money. He ran home through the streets in his underwear, black and blue from the beating. The six blocks felt the longest of trips for a bruised Esteban. The police said they would try to find the boys, but Isabella could tell the incident wasn't going to be a priority. At night, Pedro listened to the story and said, "Don't worry. I'll fix everything."

The next afternoon a boy appeared at their door. He handed over all Esteban's clothes and twice as many Euros as were taken. The boy received a mild beating, cried his apologies, and fled. After that, nothing more was said about how Pedro had recovered Esteban's clothes, or why he lived so well.

Isabella took her boy all over Rome. She loved every minute and took him to the Vatican. While there, she told him someday he too would become a priest. "That would be a great blessing," she said. "I would surely go to heaven. You want your mama to go to heaven, don't you?"

Esteban never had to answer. The answer was understood.

During the two-month stay in Rome, Isabella and Stephen hardly ever argued. Stephen treated Isabella with respect, courtesy, and understanding. She reciprocated by treating him with loving affection. But everything ended all too soon, almost the moment their connecting train left Switzerland to begin the four-hundred-kilometers to Frankfurt. As the train thundered northward, Esteban felt unsettled and nomadic. The Ferraris were met as they got off the train by a businessman and former officer from the German Bundeswehr, Retired Captain Erik ten Hag.

"Herr Ferrari, Erik ten Hag. The local office has assigned me to get you settled. Is this all your luggage? *Gut.* No need to worry about it." He turned and issued orders in German to a middle-aged man who stood right behind him.

The man replied, "*Ja*," and went about gathering the suitcases.

"Right then, just follow me," ten Hag said. "These people speak English, but I believe in speaking German to them; less chance of a misunderstanding."

He marched through the teeming and bustling train station, forcing Isabella into a trot to keep up. Parked curbside outside the main terminal, a chauffeur waited by the rear door of a large white BMW SUV. They were driven to the apartment building where they would live. They had the entire third floor and were assigned household help— a husband-and-wife team, Sebastian and Sophia Müller. The husband brought the bags into the building and up to the apartment. When everyone was inside the foyer, including Erik ten Hag, Sebastian said, "Welcome to your new home."

"You can call them Sebastian and Sophia or Herr and Frau Müller; they'll answer to either," Erik ten Hag said. "They live just upstairs. Sophia is your cook and housekeeper. Sebastian will do all the maintenance work. Okey doke, I must be off. Just call me if anything crops up." Erik ten Hag handed Stephen a business card with contact details. "Any questions before I go?"

Isabella was breathless from the speed of it all and the surprise of the lovely large apartment. There were three bedrooms, a large bath, kitchen, dining room, formal parlor, and an informal sitting room. Herr Müller placed the luggage and bags in the bedrooms, and Frau Müller asked if the family would like to eat. Sophia had taken the liberty to prepare a hearty homemade soup with barley and meatballs. They ate. Stephen announced he had work to do and left. Isabella and Esteban were left to unpack and begin settling in. The Müllers were helpful and courteous. In less than a week, Isabella and Esteban felt at home and had the lay of the land. Esteban enrolled in a Catholic secondary school three short blocks from the apartment.

Unlike when they arrived in Spain, Esteban didn't have a head start in speaking the language. But, within two months, he mastered German. The feat astounded his teachers and made the Müllers proud. From his first day in Frankfurt, Esteban asked the Müllers for certain words and phrases, and he made himself understood in only a week. In addition, when the Müllers didn't want anyone to understand what they were saying, they would switch to a Bavarian dialect. Esteban thought this was a game, and he also learned the dialect. It became their secret language. It didn't take long before Isabella fell into feeling isolated again. As with her experience in Madrid, she didn't know anyone in Frankfurt. She missed not having family around, and she became ever more protective of Esteban. This grew even worse when Signore Romero reappeared. He visited once or twice a month, staying for a single night in the spare bedroom. Esteban looked forward to his visits and the little gifts he brought. At this point, he spoke Spanish with his mother, English with his father, German at school and with the Müllers, and Italian with the Signore.

On one visit, Signore brought Esteban a special gift, a leather-bound copy of *The Ingenious Gentleman Sir Quixote of La Mancha*, better known as Don Quixote. He said they would read it together out loud and enjoy the beauty of the language, the adventure of the story, and the purity of the thoughts.

"Miguel de Cervantes was the only intelligent man Spain has ever produced. A brilliant man not motivated by greed, a great moral philosopher. Where is he now that we need him, hmm? You start by reading the first two pages, then I'll read the next two."

It would be the only book they would read together. Isabella felt it was anti-Catholic. A man fighting windmills, how silly! The following year flew by for Esteban. He was oblivious to the pipe bombings in Cologne. In the wake of a unified Germany and the terrorist attacks occurring across the Atlantic, daily life in Germany was getting better, little by little. He was committed to his studies and was wrapped up in school and church. He didn't notice the changes he was going through. He sprouted some hair on his body, and his voice grew deeper. His so-so soprano turned into a so-so baritone, and his choir seat changed too. Boys and girls were separated at school and forbidden to talk with each other. Soon after the period of adolescent change began, a class bully asserted himself upon Esteban.

Esteban never noticed how much better his lifestyle was when compared to the others in his class. Thanks to Signore Romero, his clothes were always newer and were always immaculate, thanks to Frau Müller. Sophia would bake cookies once a week and give Esteban enough to share at school. Lukas, the bully, might have been a decent enough adolescent, but his IQ hovered around the level of a rabid dog. Lukas terrorized Esteban for being what he considered a mutt —half Mexican, half American. While Esteban lived in a large apartment and had much to eat, Lukas lived in a small two-room apartment with a bathroom shared with two other families and barely had enough to eat with nothing left over and nothing to share. Stephen had become an influential businessman, while Lukas' dad had been a struggling line worker who had suffered a fatal accident when a malfunctioning robotic arm toppled over. Lukas saw Esteban as a deserving target and extorted him for money and food. Esteban never told anyone. He was afraid of the beating he might receive. One day, he had no money, and his cookies were all gone. Furious, Lukas beat the living daylights out of him. He blackened both of Esteban's eyes and bloodied his nose and mouth. He ripped the boy's jacket, shirt, and pants but decided to take his shoes rather than trash them. Isabella was outraged. Stephen was in Vienna and wouldn't be home for a few days. She didn't know what to do, so she called her brother in Italy. Pedro listened and got as angry as Isabella. "I'm helpless to help you," he said. "I have no friends in Frankfurt to ask for a favor."

By the time Stephen got home, Isabella was mad as hell, a Mount Vesuvius of rage on the verge of eruption. She lit into Stephen and raged at him for two hours, non-stop. This was accompanied by repetitive slamming of the bedroom door. Finally, Stephen said, "I'll take care of it. I'll take care of it." He took a business card out of his wallet and called Erik ten Hag.

The next afternoon, when Esteban got home from school, his father and two non-commissioned German officers wearing red berets greeted him. Following introductions, the Wachtmeister took control immediately.

"Young man, you will call me 'Wachtmeister,' and this gentleman, you will address as 'Korporal.' You will also call us 'Sir.' We will be der 'Herr Wachtmeister' and der 'Herr Korporal.' Starting today, we will teach you how to defend yourself. Is that clear? Right! Go change your clothes."

Four months later, Esteban's instruction was complete. Once again, Esteban found himself in a situation where he had neither money nor cookies, and Lukas started his assault with a punch to the face. Esteban blocked the blow and hit back with two short blows to the stomach. Lukas stepped back enraged, then charged headfirst at Esteban like a bull. Esteban accepted the charge and threw Lukas eight feet into a cinderblock wall. Lukas broke his nose as he fell, got up, and turned for another lunge. This time, Esteban stepped inside and hit him in the mouth so hard he broke two teeth. Lukas slumped to the ground holding his face and screaming. The sight of his own blood caused terror and panic. Scrambling to his feet, he ran home, while Esteban picked up the chipped teeth and walked home to show the Wachtmeister his trophy.

The Wachtmeister said, "Right. Your instruction is over. Now, you must never start a fight or provoke one. You have been taught defense, not offense. Remember this."

Lukas never bothered Esteban again; he even sought to befriend him the following year. Isabella and Stephen had to go and see the priest at their son's school. They both expected to be reprimanded for the beating Lukas received. Instead, the father thanked them as well as Esteban for making things right. Isabella was angry at Esteban for straying from God's ways, while Stephen was proud of his son for standing up to be a man. After thanking God that Lukas had been put in his place, the father said, "But we can't allow the boy to think his behavior is acceptable. We'll have to punish Esteban." As an afterthought added, "And Lukas for instigating the fight."

Stephen thought this was wrong and complained about the morality of punishing his son for defending himself. Isabella immediately recognized an opportunity to correct her husband's error in judgment from what she believed to be true. She interrupted Stephen and gave the father permission to punish Esteban. He was punished by having to say a whole rosary each day for two weeks. When he asked the priest what penance Lukas had for his part in the fight. The priest brushed it away by saying, "It's been dealt with, and besides, losing two teeth was punishment enough."

Pleased with his son, Stephen spoke about doing man things. He wanted his son to participate in more sports, which meant playing soccer and getting laid. Isabella was against the latter and appalled that Stephen would even say such a thing. Stephen would ask Esteban, "How are you doing with the girls? Got any in trouble?" and he would laugh. Stephen would say to Isabella, "Leave the goddam kid alone. Let him be a man." He'd said these things before, but now they were more intense and with more emotion. Isabella held her ground.

"Don't be like your father. Do as I say," she would plead.

Esteban was confused. Life was almost bearable when his dad wasn't home. But the messaging became confusing and contradictory when he was. His dad was the original swaggering jackass. At least, that was the name his mother called Stephen when she thought Esteban couldn't hear her.

She accused Stephen of being unfaithful.

"What of it," he would say. "I'm not getting any from you!"

This would go on for years. His father taunted him to be a man and used himself as an exemplary role model. His mother pleaded with Esteban to follow Jesus' example and warned him of the perils of hell if he didn't. His mother had more control of his day-to-day affairs and kept a tight leash on her boy. Something would have to give.

It did when Esteban reached sixteen.

CHAPTER 5

EMMA

At sixteen, he was handsome. His hair was dark and curly, his skin was light and clear with no signs of teenage acne. While his eyes were hazel, they could appear greenish or even blue depending on the light. He wasn't demure by any stretch of the imagination; his manner bore a rough easiness. The roughness could have been attributed to the awkwardness of most teenage boys, but with Esteban, it was an attempt to imitate his father. The easiness came from his mother and her constant reminders to go in God's way and to be like their savior, the Lord Jesus Christ.

Esteban rarely tried to get his own way. But whenever the slightest bit of aggression surfaced, there was always someone on hand who cared for him, his mother, his father, Signore Romero, Frau Müller, or a priest. From practice, he learned to speed through a Rosary in under thirty-five minutes. How much under thirty-five minutes depended on the prayer language. Latin turned out to be the fastest as it contained the fewest words.

In school, Esteban's grades were average. His weakest spot was mathematics. He failed calculus and had to be tutored. Catechism was his standout subject, which made his priest teachers and mother radiate with pride.

"Esteban," the priest asked. "What is the chief end of man?"

"To glorify God and enjoy Him forever!" Esteban replied.

His affinity for language was well-established. He was now fluent in English, Italian, Spanish, German, and Latin. In addition, Esteban would soon become fluent in French, which he picked up from another expatriate. Thierry Henri lived in the same apartment building and called Quebec home. If languages could be considered a game, Esteban was an impressive player.

When it came to girls, Esteban was beyond timid, especially when it came to Emma Lewandowski. She was a year older and in her final year—whether or not she passed her exams. She was mature for her age, as was her whole generation, who had grown up in a country anticipating the next Al-Qaeda-sponsored attack. She had intense teal-blue eyes. Her hair was silvery blonde, which she always wore with pigtails. To say her body was perfect would be an understatement, but her mind was the epitome of an airhead poster child. She was also promiscuous. She was oversexed, and everyone knew it. Everyone except Esteban.

Esteban fell head over heels in love with her in the most secretive way. He dreamed about her. He fantasized about her. He woke up from having a dream about her and found his underwear and sheets icky. He was deathly afraid his mother would find out and punish him, but Frau Müller cleaned everything up and never said a word. He felt guilty about his feelings for Emma and confessed to all the impure thoughts he had in his head and the impure sensations he felt in his loins. The father confessor said this was a terrible sin and asked if Esteban had ever masturbated. When he shook his head and whispered, "No," the priest told him he could still be saved but, nonetheless, made sure his penance was excessive and harsh.

At the Pope Benedict XVI school, the boys weren't allowed to speak with or have any contact with the girls. They had separate everything, including school hours and lunchtimes. The girls' school day began thirty minutes earlier to reduce the chances of contact. The fathers and sisters listened to the students' conversations to ensure they weren't talking about the opposite gender and that most heinous of subjects, sex. The boys would leave home an hour early under the pretense of attending Mass. Likewise, the girls would often find reasons to stay late after school. The students learned to adjust what they were saying mid-sentence should a person dressed in black pass within earshot. An erudite female student might switch to a phrase such as, "The sister's history class on Joan of Arc was riveting. I felt like I was actually there!" or a male student might let it be known that, "The reverend father really helped me to understand economic pressures on policy measures." Those dressed in black began to believe the praises being heaped upon them and found themselves having to confess to the sin of vanity.

Emma always found a reason to stay late at school. Of course, from her perspective, she'd graduate at the end of the semester—from boys to men! Later, she would go on to meet an army second lieutenant. He was 82nd Airborne, a wholesome American mama's boy from below the Mason-Dixon Line. The family had bought his education and became overjoyed when he joined the army with a commission. At first, the family remained skeptical when he told them he was in love with a German girl. However, they changed their minds after flying to Germany to meet her. Emma came across as pleasant and suitable for their son. They were also convinced she wasn't marrying their son for his money. In all honesty, she wasn't. He would be the only man in her life who didn't tell her she was stupid. They would live happily ever after, and the family trust fund served to protect them from themselves.

The only thing all the boys talked about was the girls at the school. The girl most often discussed was Emma. She knew it, and she liked it. She also liked Lukas. She liked many boys, but Lukas was the most aggressive, and he appeared the most mature. Esteban never spoke to her or any other girls, so she thought something was wrong with him. Lukas kept trying to be friends with Esteban and to persuade him to come to school early for no other reason than to talk with the girls. Esteban mentioned that he usually arrived early to school, which was true. But Esteban being Esteban, arriving early was the only way to attend the early morning Mass. The priests said it was wrong to talk to the girls, so he didn't despite the urging of Lukas and the other boys. However, Esteban found himself listening to the conversations about the girls. He listened to his peers brag about their exploits.

"I had my hands on those jugs!"

"I had my hands under her blouse and on her doorknobs!" another said.

Someone else sounded like a crowing rooster. "I had her blouse off, and those boobs cupped in my hands!"

On and on this would go, with each boy trying to one-up the other until Lukas exclaimed, "Nailed it!"

Lukas' boast would shut everyone up, and draw looks of both respect and envy. As the school year plowed on, more and more of the conversations ended with some form of triumphant claim. Whenever one of the boys made this final boast, there was an unbridled acceptance into some sort of secret society from which Esteban found himself excluded. Esteban was under tremendous peer pressure to prove himself a man. This pressure wasn't confined to school.

At home, Stephen became concerned about his son's sexuality, saying it was unnatural for a boy his age to have no interest in girls. Esteban had plenty of interest in girls but didn't talk about it because his mother would go crazy. Conversations about girls turned into nasty arguments, with his father exclaiming louder than a Harley 883 Bobber, "For Christ's sake, let the kid be a man. Let him get laid."

Full throttled, Isabella screeched. "Don't you dare be like your father." Per usual, she slammed the bedroom door.

Esteban made up his mind. He would be a man, get laid, prove himself to his father, and win his unconditional love. Given time, his mother would find it in her heart to forgive him. At least, that's what he hoped. So, he'd agree the next time Lukas offered to fix him up, he would accept. Sure enough, it wasn't long before Lukas made the offer. Lukas clapped him on the back and said, "I know just the one for you."

The next day Lukas met up with Esteban and told him,

"Emma thinks you're nice. If you ask her to the multiplex, she'll go."

For the remainder of the day, Lukas helped him build up his confidence. After school, the two found themselves face to face. This was the most beautiful girl Esteban had ever seen and of whom he had dreamed for so long, and he now found himself downright tongue-tied. He not only couldn't speak, but he also couldn't breathe. Lukas kept on prodding him until Esteban finally blurted, "Do... do... you... you... w... wa... want to... to g... g... gggo to... to... to the moo... moo... movies Sa... Sat... Saturday arf... afterno... noon?"

After she nodded and smiled, they discussed the necessary details. Esteban spent the rest of the week in a state of happy delirium, such was his anticipation. This feeling was juxtaposed by a euphoric deflating concern over what he would say when his mother found out. Lukas and the other boys talked about how lucky he was to go out with Emma. "She has the most beautiful bazookas and really likes it," they'd say. Esteban acted with indifference, while inside, he was seething with self-doubt.

How am I going to get away? he wondered. Frau Müller came to his rescue, and she would tell Isabella he was visiting friends. One day followed the next. Finally, D-Day arrived. Esteban did all his usual Saturday morning things, including going to confession with Isabella. Only this Saturday, he avoided the confessional by telling Isabella he'd gone yesterday, which he hadn't because he didn't want the priest to give him a penance.

At 1:30 p.m., he rang the bell to Emma's apartment, and she immediately opened the door. At first, he didn't recognize her. Her hair was combed out and let down instead of her usual pigtails. She wore make-up and a dress tailored to her body's shape. Her beauty took his breath away, and he couldn't move. He couldn't talk. He couldn't do anything. Finally, she grabbed his hand and said, "Come in." He walked in stiff-legged.

Emma's apartment was typical. There were several rooms around a parlor with a bathroom down the hall. The building and the apartment were in impeccable condition. She led Esteban to the living room and invited him to sit on her big, overstuffed sofa. He sank into the cushions and felt awkward. She sat down next to him.

"My parents won't be home for a while. Would you prefer to stay here?" she asked.

Stammering, he said, "Uh huh."

If only he had said, "No!" If only he insisted, they go to the movies. All these ifs. He stayed. Esteban spent years trying to forget and denying what occurred over the next ninety minutes.

He tried, but he couldn't. Emma did all she could to help him. She undressed in front of him, and then she undressed him. She kissed him and touched him, but all to no avail. He couldn't. He was far too nervous. He was far too shy. He was far too timid. He was far too scared. He was far too afraid of not passing Go, not collecting $200, and going straight to hell. No matter how hard he tried, he couldn't get aroused. And wham! A miracle. Emma wasted no time at all. Then, faster than Road Runner zipping passed Wile E. Coyote, she pulled him on top of her. But before he could penetrate her, he climaxed. He was aghast and humiliated. Emma was furious. She felt rejected. She tried to get him aroused again. At first with sweet words. When that failed, she used harsh demands.

None of her unrelenting efforts worked. Esteban was to the point of tears because of his shame. She was to the point of tears because of her frustration. This was the first time something like this had happened to her! This was the first time anything like this had happened to him!

"What kind of man are you?" she asked.

She belittled him. She told him to get dressed and to get out. She would get a boy who knew what to do, someone like Lukas. At three o'clock, he stood on the sidewalk in front of Emma's apartment, shunned and humiliated beyond belief. Worse, he had no one to talk to about the experience. He couldn't tell his father for fear of his dad's adverse reaction. He couldn't tell his mother. She would have a fit and spend hours banging the bedroom door and cursing at his father. He couldn't tell the priests. In all likelihood, the priests would say he would no longer be allowed into heaven and that even purgatory was too good for him. He was condemned to spend the rest of eternity in hell. How could he even contemplate confessing? The penance would make his past penances pale by comparison. He couldn't tell his friends. They were all successful and bragged about being a man.

Over the course of the following week, he lived with the persistent fear that somebody would find out. He was afraid she would tell someone, anyone, and everyone. Emma would tell no one. She wanted no one to find out she couldn't arouse him, afraid it would make others doubt her beauty and sexuality. This whole experience wouldn't make any difference in six months, and she would forget about Esteban.

Lukas wanted Esteban to share the intimate details. Esteban didn't answer, and Lukas took his blank grin as a knowing smile. Lukas slapped him on the back and shook his hand. The other boys now accepted him into the secret society of manhood. He knew he didn't belong in this society and took on shame and guilt. For many months after his frightful experience, he noticed he no longer had erections. But he couldn't stop thinking about what had happened, and his thoughts consumed him.

If Esteban had someone to speak with, they could have assured him that first-time experiences aren't always heavenly. He felt something was wrong with him, and shortly before his seventeenth birthday, he concluded he'd have nothing to do with women. His experience with Emma must have been a divine sign. He would take this signal as a final call to embrace celibacy and dedicate his life to serving the Lord. A great weight had been lifted from his shoulders and from his soul. He announced his decision to become a priest at home and school on the same day.

As you can well imagine, his mother was over the moon, beyond ecstatic. Stephen was the complete opposite. The priests at his school were overjoyed. Finally, one of their students would join their order. He would attend a beautiful seminary in Rome.

"Esteban Ferrari had the calling," they said to each other.

Because he was considered a devout Catholic and a satisfactory student in most subjects, his paperwork was processed with haste. As a result, his enrollment in the seminary would begin in a matter of weeks.

Signore Romero visited the family around the time Esteban was due to leave. His last words to Esteban were, "Things are not always as they seem. Think about it."

Esteban never saw the Signore again. In future years, Esteban would read on the Internet how the Signore was an innocent bystander in a terrorist attack in Tunisia. Other news reports placed the Signore closer to the situation as someone who played an integral part in a group smuggling contraband.

Isabella spent Esteban's remaining time in Frankfurt celebrating. Stephen spent his remaining time inebriated.

CHAPTER 6

JESUS

The building was old. Very old. It was one of the many old religious buildings spared during the multitude of brutal wars of the twentieth century. Used as student living quarters, it doubled as an initiation area for those seeking to learn how to live the Life of Christ. Truth be told, the abbot wouldn't have minded if the building got razed. A newer building would need far less upkeep. Even in a Mediterranean climate, the cold harbored inside antiquated walls. The Vatican, mindful of the situation, wanted to emphasize building new shrines and classrooms.

Esteban was ill-prepared for this type of dwelling. He was assigned to share a room with three other first-year postulants. Each boy was older than Esteban, and the oldest, a twenty-year-old, assumed the role of the room's leader. The room had two armoires, two desks, and two bunk beds. Everything had to be shared. For clothes, the postulants received hand-me-downs from upperclassmen. The uniform was comprised of a white shirt, which had to be clean at all times, black pants, a black jacket, and a Roman collar. The jackets were adorned with a small cross of Jesus on the right lapel. The color of the cross served to denote the year of study. Students in their last year donned a red one. The red crosses thought nothing of hazing everyone else. In turn, they were bullied by their teachers, whether they were priests or brothers. For now, Esteban wore a blue cross. Those wearing blue crosses were relegated to errand and whipping boy status.

Esteban never realized what an easy life his parents had afforded him. He had a doting and protective mother and a father who made sure there was always enough money for food and clean clothes. Granted, his parents' constant bickering and his father's extended business trips weren't particularly easy, but this new life was altogether another kettle of fish.

The oldest roommate was Brother Sergey. Sergey grew up along the border of Poland and Belarus and had become accustomed to hearing a constant rat-tat-tat of machine guns from the surrounding forests. Brother János was Hungarian, and Brother Milan was from Luxembourg. The school curriculum would be taught in Latin and Italian. Regardless, everyone in the room would have long adjustment periods.

Esteban would have the most challenging adjustment of the quartet even though he became an interpreter and language coach for his roommates. His help stopped them from further bullying him as the youngest. Sergey turned out to be politically astute, and these skills allowed him to sidetrack the more challenging tasks assigned to postulants. Growing up in and around hostile areas, he learned what it took to survive. But he wasn't open to sharing this knowledge. He knew from experience that to share insight was to lose its benefits. Some of the more experienced teachers were wise to Sergey but chose to ignore his transgressions so long as the other students didn't contravene.

The first three weeks were hectic with everyone trying to settle into their new routine. Rumors abounded about everything and anything. Even in the seminary, sex was a significant topic of discussion among the students, even though they all knew the subject was taboo and a mortal sin, let alone its practice. The good fathers knew of the talk, which was a foremost concern. "We must teach them the pious way," they said during their meetings and discussed harsh penances and punishments. That was one point of unified concurrence —the discipline had to be severe.

The abbot repeated his favorite expression, "Before the building comes the foundation." The foundation was a strict regimen accounting for every waking hour. For centuries, military armies used similar techniques to train recruits, and the monks had long adopted corporal punishment and mind games to break down each and every postulant.

Keeping the initiates tired was important as was seclusion. There were no visitations for the first six months. They would be permitted to receive letters but were not sanctioned to get gifts or text messages. Esteban lost weight and became homesick. He thought everyone was out to get him, and he was right. He wanted to drop out, but he couldn't quit. How would he be able to face his mother? She would be so ashamed. She would also guilt him into thinking his decision would prevent her from entering heaven. His father would laugh him out of the house. Even in the classroom, where Esteban had good moments, the teachers had a way of belittling his answers and making him feel inferior. All part of the mind games to break down a postulant.

"If you're so smart," they said, "you should do more and do better." But, for some reason, he couldn't find a way to get the answers right. The abbot had another mantra he liked repeating. "No mercy for anyone. They get it right, or they get out. The foundation must be solid."

The summer months were warm, and the close quarters were hot. Esteban couldn't talk with his roommates because they didn't appear to be having any trouble, and compared to him, that was true. Thanks to Esteban, his roommates were learning the languages they needed, but in helping them, he couldn't find a way to help himself. For whatever reason, Sergey, János, and Milan felt no undue obligation to assist him. He lived each day in outright terror. He had no friends. None whatsoever. He thought things couldn't get any worse. He thought about killing himself. He knew he would go straight to hell for committing suicide, but he no longer cared.

After a particularly bad day, he walked back to his room, contemplating how his death would solve all his unsolvable problems, when he heard a voice. "Not a good idea."

Esteban looked around but saw no one. He kept walking and returned to his depression. He began to cry; tears rolled down his cheeks. He wept, "I want to be alone."

"No place to hide?" the voice asked.

Esteban stopped dead in his tracks and looked around. But, again, he saw no one. He walked on, clinging tight to his depressed state of mind.

The voice continued. "Even if you could hide, you know they'd find you."

"Who's talking to me?" Esteban asked.

"Me," the voice said.

Esteban looked around again and saw no one.

"Who's talking to me? Where are you?"

"I'm right next to you."

Sure enough, walking right next to Esteban was a dark-skinned youngster dressed much like Esteban, including the collar and a blue cross.

"Who are you? I've never seen you before," Esteban said.

"I've been here the whole time," the boy said.

Esteban looked hard at the boy. His long wavy hair covered his ears and fell over his collar, reaching down past his shoulder blade.

"You can't be," Esteban said. "Your hair is too long. They'd make you cut it."

"They made a special exemption for me." The boy laughed. Esteban looked the boy over again.

"You're wearing sandals," Esteban said.

"More comfortable than those heavy shoes."

"How are you allowed to get away with that?" Esteban asked.

"Dispensation."

"What's your name?"

"You won't believe me," the boy answered.

"Sure, I will. What's your name?"

"Jesus," was the answer.

"Come on, what's your name?" Esteban asked.

"I told you!"

Esteban was quiet for a few steps. "Are you Hispanic?" he asked in Spanish. "I know a few Hispanics named Jesus. But they pronounce it *Hey-zeus*."

In Spanish, the boy replied, "No, I'm not Spanish, and it's

fine if they say *Hey-zeus*. I won't reject someone for their pronunciation or for using the wrong name. Languages change over time and from one location to the next. Even the current spelling of my name didn't come about until long after the King James Bible was printed. Listen, you can call me anything you want as long as it's not late for meals. Speaking of food, isn't it about time for supper?"

Esteban realized he was hungry for the first time in weeks. "I guess. What do you think they're having?"

"What difference does it make? A good appetite makes for good food. Let's go eat," Jesus said.

Esteban and his newfound friend went off for their first supper together.

With little room available at the dining table, Esteban had to sit on his books. One of the monks said, "You can't learn anything from sitting on your books." The other boys all laughed.

Jesus said to Esteban, "That's the only way I ever learned anything," and laughed at the monk.

Esteban smiled but restrained himself from laughing for fear of angering the monk. Jesus' quip removed the sting of the monk's comment and the boys' laughter.

After dinner, Esteban asked, "Where're you from?"

"Bethlehem."

"Bethlehem?"

"Right. Listen, I've got to go and study. I'll see you later." Jesus went off, leaving Esteban to face the night alone.

Over the next several days, Jesus would show up whenever Esteban was having a tough time, and that was quite often. One morning, Esteban committed a minor crime in the classroom. He dropped one of his books on the floor, and it landed with such a loud bang that it startled everyone in the room, including the monk teaching the prayers. Although it was an accident, the monk thought otherwise. Esteban received a caning for his insolence. The beating hurt physically and emotionally, and he spent the rest of the day crying and limping around. After the school day, he shuffled back to his quarters when Jesus showed up and said, "Tough day, huh?"

Esteban didn't answer, and Jesus didn't expect one. He continued. "You're not getting the idea."

"What do you know?" Esteban shot back in a tone that would have sent a dog scampering.

"Enough. I wasn't always Jesus, you know."

"Who were you?" Esteban asked, surprised by the comment.

"Little Ban Ban and sometimes, Hey Kid. It wasn't easy for me either until I learned."

"Learned what?" Esteban asked.

"To keep my mouth shut. But listen to me. To get along, you have to go along. In time, my time came along, and so will yours."

"I don't understand," Esteban said

"Of course not. But you will," Jesus said. Without pausing, he continued. "When I was born, everyone said I had such great promise. Blah, blah, blah, blah. My parents didn't want to hear about any of this. To them, I was like all the other babies, in constant need of nursing and always having to have my swaddling changed. Worse still, because of me, they had to keep moving. I was a real fast learner, and that only attracted more attention. My mother wanted me to become a shepherd. My father thought being a stonemason would be right up my alley. I wanted to be rich. Everyone wants to be rich, am I right?"

"And then what?" Esteban asked.

"After my Bar Mitzvah, it was time to be apprenticed. I got hooked up with the Essenes. They lived out in the desert and told my parents they would teach me. I'm telling you, I thought I'd gone to heaven. I was so happy to be free of my folks. If I had only known what a strict lifestyle those guys led. All the time, it was, 'don't do this,' 'don't do that.' Study. Study. Study. Work. Work. Work. Study. Work. They were the ones who turned me onto carpentry. I hated that part. All the sawdust, the stuff gets into every crevice. But from the experience, I took away one critical thing: there's a time and place for everything. A season for everything. I learned to be patient. I learned to go along so I could get along. It was hard. Real hard. But I learned, and so can you."

"What do I have to do?" Esteban asked.

"Accept what is happening and what you are. Stop fighting the surroundings and the discipline. You can't change them. Trust me on this. I couldn't," Jesus answered.

Over the next few weeks, Esteban took Jesus' advice to heart, and he adjusted. He walked humbly. He became very pious. He did all he was told without a word. He accepted his lot in life. As far as the teachers were concerned, he had been broken. The foundation was at last ready for the building. Seven months into the first year and Esteban was now seeing things their way. "He's ready to become a disciple," the priests informed the abbot.

The next few months were easier. Isabella flew into Rome's Leonardo da Vinci International Airport, and Esteban was allowed to visit with her and Pedro. He learned what prayers to say wherever he walked, so the monks thought he was in constant prayer.

Jesus said, "Now you're getting it."

One day, a monk asked Esteban, "You are doing very well, my son. Who has helped you?"

Without missing a beat, Esteban answered, "Jesus."

The monk reported this answer to the abbot. The abbot smiled and said, "He is a true believer. Jesus helps us all."

He was no longer a whipping boy. His teachers no longer scorned or belittled him. They decided he might make a good monk after all. He would be invited to join the order. He had accepted his surroundings and his surroundings accepted him. The year was almost over. The talk now was of what the second year would bring. The postulants spoke in their native languages inside their quarters, and Esteban joked with them all. Sergey had taught Esteban enough Polish to be conversant, and Esteban had taught Sergey enough Italian to make him fluent. Next year would be all right. Esteban would be able to handle it. Everything in the seminary was familiar. While joking with his roommates, the abbot was reading a letter to his immediate staff.

"So, that's the net of it," said the abbot. "The Pope wants us to take our twenty best postulants and send them to the Gregorian Seminary. We're going to have to comply. Who shall we send?"

"Why do we have to comply?" the old monk who taught Latin and Greek asked.

The abbot reminded everyone, "At present, the number of new priests is at an all-time low. The Pope has made a humble request for our assistance. The Pope is not known to make humble requests. When he does, it's in our best interest to comply. Let's not forget we are in desperate need of upgrading our facilities. I'd like to think His Holiness will look upon us with kindness when we comply."

The old monk nodded. "In that case, Reverend Father, we must send our very best. The Gregorians insist on only taking the smartest and the most pious. Thus, we must select those who will not only do well but also look back at us and remember us. Let us consider this as sowing grain. The best seeds grow the best crop."

The room was silent. Everyone understood the threat and the promise. Compliance meant the promise of regained esteem from the Pope and the hope the Pope would forget past disagreements. Halfhearted compliance or noncompliance held the threat of ostracism and a future of denied requests.

"I can think of three young men who will represent us with honor," the old monk said. For the next two hours, a list of names was put forth and discussed. Finally, everyone agreed on which twenty names should go on the list. The first thing the following morning, a brother entered Esteban's shared quarters and said, "Brother Sergey, Brother Milan, please go to the Office of the Abbot. The Reverend Father and the old monk wish to speak with you."

Brother Sergey and Brother Milan looked at each other, and fear showed in their eyes. *What now?* was their simultaneous worried thought.

With much trepidation, they hurried off to see the abbot. Brother János and Esteban wondered what was going on and felt apprehensive. Many others shared that same apprehension throughout the day and into the evening.

"What did they want?" Brother János asked.

"They want us to go to the Gregorian seminary," said Brother Milan.

Brother János grew excited. "That's the top college for priests. Why did they ask you and not us?"

"I don't know!" Brother Sergey answered. "Why don't you go ask them?"

Brother János slumped into a chair. Esteban shook both brothers' hands and congratulated them. "Good. Good." He smiled. "I'll miss you."

Brother Sergey was smiling.

Brother Milan was not. "I don't know if I want to go," he said.

"Not go! Not go! How could you not want to go?" Esteban asked. "You have to go. That is the order."

"If you don't go, will you please tell them I want to go?" Brother János said.

Milan didn't reply.

The following day, Brother Milan woke earlier than usual, said morning prayers, and went to see the old monk. The old monk would understand. Before lunch, the old monk went to the abbot.

"What do you mean he doesn't want to go?" the abbot asked.

"Reverend Father, he wishes to become a monk. He has no desire to be a priest. He says he wishes to devote his life to God by tending our vines and making our brandy. He seeks the quiet life of prayer and contemplation," the old monk answered.

"Who will we send in his place? We must send twenty appointees as wished by the Holy Father."

"I have one other name that might do. He's pious and has

a gift for language. He's proving to be my best pupil in both Latin and Greek."

"Who is this?" the abbot asked.

"Brother Esteban."

"Ah, yes! He's the one who says Jesus helps him. He is pious enough, but I thought we were going to ask him to become a brother in our order?" the abbot said.

"That is true. We could nominate Esteban to the Gregorians and have Brother Milan join us. That should please everyone," the old monk said.

"What kind of student do you think he will be with the Gregorians?"

"Not the best, but good enough. He won't be a leader, but Brother Sergey will be there. Sergey will be a leader. And we'll still be able to tell His Holiness we are sending our very best." The old monk smiled.

"A practical approach, as always." The abbot smiled back.

When Brother János found out, he wailed, "You! You!" Being disappointed, he went on. "I'm smarter than you." He wagged his finger at Brother Esteban. He turned and faced Milan. "It's all your fault! Why didn't you tell them to send me? I wanted to go."

"It's not in our hands," Brother Sergey said, trying to quiet Brother János, who turned and stormed out of the room in a huff, realizing it was a useless argument.

Brother Sergey turned to Brother Esteban and said, "We'd better get packed. We have to leave tomorrow."

Before they left, Brother Esteban was called to see the old monk one last time.

"Brother Esteban, you need to know a few things before

leaving," the old monk said. Brother Esteban nodded and listened.

"You weren't our first choice. In truth, if Brother Milan had not withdrawn, you would have stayed with us. The Gregorian seminary can be challenging. Only the best graduates go on to become priests. You'll have to work hard. But, if you find things too difficult, you'll always have a place in our order as a friar. May God bless you."

"How do you like them apples?" Jesus asked as they walked away.

"What do you mean?"

"He told you that he doesn't expect you to make it with the Gregorians."

"Maybe I won't," Esteban said.

"Not with that attitude, you won't," Jesus said.

"What do you mean?"

"The Essenes didn't expect me to last either," Jesus said. "I found out they even took bets, which, ironically, is against their creed. But I fooled them. I fooled myself, too. You might not finish first, but you can finish. And that's what I did."

"Will you help me?" Esteban asked.

"Will you help yourself?"

"I'll try."

"Try! How do you try to help yourself? You either help yourself, or you don't," Jesus said.

"You're right. I'll help myself," Esteban said after a thoughtful pause.

"That's good," Jesus said. "Let's hurry. The bus is waiting."

CHAPTER 7

GREGORIANS

The Gregorian seminary was located a handful of miles away. However, the real distance between the two seminaries was immeasurable. Its buildings were a mixture of old and new, and even the old buildings looked to be in good order. A new building was underway with an army of students pitching in to help the workers. The school's aura was different. Lighter and even brighter.

"Good afternoon, my name is Father Peter," a smiling priest said. "My responsibility is to look after your temporal wellbeing. The courses here are designed to be difficult. Many of you won't make it through to the priesthood. The competition will be tough, but you have been selected as the best candidates from your nominating seminaries. If ever you find yourself needing help, please come and see me. We want you to be as comfortable as possible. If you have no questions, I will hand you your room assignments."

By the luck of the draw, Sergey and Esteban were to be roommates again. Brother Sergey was quite happy with the arrangement, and, under his breath, he said to Esteban in an American accent, "Welcome to SEAL Team 6."

Esteban was confused by his meaning.

During the course of Esteban's first year at the Gregorian seminary, the physical discipline wasn't arduous in any shape or form. On the contrary, compared to his prior seminary, it was effortless. Penances were easy or non-existent. Esteban felt conflicted and confused. When he or his friends transgressed in some minor way, the brothers and priests would treat the incident with an unexpected *laissez-faire* attitude. The Gregorian priests' viewpoint was, boys will be boys!

Their venial sins were treated almost as if they weren't sins at all, earning sinners one or two Hail Marys or Our Fathers. Mortal sins, on the other hand, were a different ball game. If a sin were connected with sex and had wormed itself past an impure thought, there would be fire and brimstone. If a student had an impure thought, committed an act, caused somebody else to commit an act, and enjoyed the act, they would be given a front-row seat into a full-time experience of living in hell. One of the fathers gave a teaching sermon where he compared masturbation to murder and suicide. Many of the students thought this might be a stretch. Still, through constant indoctrination, the students adopted similar attitudes and adapted their moral philosophies. The priests were pleased to watch the novices' progress.

The mental discipline was brutal, albeit subtle. Father Peter was true to his welcoming words. The courses were indeed difficult. Every student learned what study meant. A disciplined procedure of study, study, study. Recite. Demonstrate. Study, study, study. Esteban thought his head would break open. He was going crazy from all the hard work. He complained to Jesus.

Jesus sympathized with him but said, "Stop complaining!"

Halfway through the year, Esteban sat in the chapel with a crushing migraine. By the skin of his teeth, he'd passed an important mid-term examination. Although he'd scraped by, his knew grades weren't high enough to make the cut to continue with the junior year.

"What am I going to do?" he asked.

"About what?" Jesus said.

"About staying in this school. I don't think I'll make the cut. I wish I were as smart as Sergey. He's not having any trouble. Worse, he makes me feel stupid." Esteban was in another cantankerous mood.

"The first thing you can do is stop whining. Whenever anyone asks how you are, you whine in such a way that nobody believes you. I don't."

"Really?" Esteban replied. He was taken aback by the accusation.

"Whine, whine, whine. Complain, complain, complain. Cut it out already. It's drawing negative attention upon yourself. You're acting like a Greek tragedy. The gods are not out to get you. Only the priests and the brothers! And you can beat them at their own game."

"Did you have the same problem?" Esteban asked.

"Why do you think I know to tell you all this? When I was living with the Essenes, I also took to feeling sorry for myself. It was an arduous life. Rabbi Johanan ben Zakkai told me the story of the Greek gods. Do you know it?"

"No," said Esteban. "Our history lessons start with the Romans. What about the Greek gods?"

Jesus began. "The Greek gods could be a nasty bunch. Quite a vengeful lot. Once they disliked you, they'd go out of their way to make your life miserable. They turned mischief-making into a pleasure sport. They would initiate a test upon some mortal based on the tiniest provocation. The mortal would reel under the pressure and fail. This failure would make the gods snarl, and they would look to start heaping on all types of trials and tribulations. So, as you'd expect, the mortals continued to fail, and the gods grew angry. That's what's happening here. When a weakness is sensed, the brothers and the priests work on it. So, by complaining, you're saying to them, 'I'm weak. Please, please, please, won't you pick on me?'"

Looking straight into Esteban's eyes, Jesus concluded, "I had to learn to keep quiet. I've already told you this. Never let them know what you think. They don't want you to think. Only tell them what they tell you." Jesus stopped talking and shrugged his shoulders.

"Is that what Sergey is doing?" Esteban asked after a few minutes of thought. "Telling the priests what they told him?"

"What do you think?" Jesus smiled.

"Hey, I thought you said not to think?" Esteban asked.

"By Jove, you're starting to get the idea. It's an article of faith. Trust me on this, kid. Let's go for supper, I'm hungry, and there's veal tonight. Mmm, mmm, mmm, my favorite." And with that, the two friends went off to dinner.

The next day, Esteban attended a challenging session. The teaching brother began asking the class questions. He turned to Esteban and asked him a difficult question. Using the same skills used when learning a new language, Esteban answered by mimicking the brother's words. Esteban made no real effort to understand the meaning of the words, but he paid attention to getting them in the right order. The brother was pleased with the answer and asked why it was so.

Esteban thought for a second and said, "It's an article of faith."

"That's right. Good." The pleased brother smiled. "And who told you that was so?"

Esteban didn't hesitate with his answer. "Jesus told me. And, believe me, I trust him on this!"

For the moment, it felt like the oxygen had been sucked out of the classroom. The brother squinted his eyes at Esteban and searched for any signal indicating his response was some type of prank. Instead, he could only see a young man who returned his stare with an open expression. He took Esteban's look for a sincere belief in his answer. The brother's smile widened as the oxygen reentered the classroom. "Excellent, Esteban," he said, turning his attention to another student with another question.

At the end of the class, the brother noted Esteban's answer in his grade book. The rest of Esteban's day was filled with similar circumstances and the same results. He continued the practice and, over the next few weeks, noticed more than a subtle change in the attitudes toward him. His grades improved, and he got called on less and less as other students fell under the baleful gaze of the instructors. In two months, he achieved the curious anonymity students seek as a form of protection. He was getting by without getting any heat.

Chalk another one up for Jesus, Esteban thought. He mentioned his improvements when he next saw Jesus. "Things have gotten a lot better! Hooyah!"

"You might want to hold off blowing your own trumpet. You're not out of the desert yet," Jesus said.

"What do you mean, not out of the desert?" Esteban asked.

"You still have much to learn and haven't scraped the surface. You're still dealing with the basics and facing the prospect of spending many years in the desert. At best, you're only on a small oasis. When I first learned your lesson, I thought I was a know-it-all too. But, in truth, I paid my dues and spent many years in the wilderness. There's a lot to learn about dealing with the heat. It's not going to get any easier any time soon."

"What do you mean?" Esteban asked.

"You'll see," Jesus answered.

"I don't think I want to."

"You're whining again," Jesus said. "You don't have any choice. Your feet are on the path. You're on a journey to change the world. You can't stop moving, so get ready. Be like a Boy Scout—be prepared."

"Prepared for what?"

"To reach your God-given potential," Jesus said.

A competitive environment led to an air of atmospheric tension. As the last few weeks of his sophomore year drew to a close, the air was thick with anticipation and anxiety. Those few, those proud, those elite students at the top of their class strutted around the seminary as if they owned the place. They found themselves becoming the objects of sermons, not of praise, but of the ego's trappings leading to the sin of pride.

Brother Sergey would finish first in his class. He had the advantage of learning the lessons of invisibility during his years in the rough-n-tumble villages of Eastern Poland. Sergey used his honed skills to avoid any negative attention upon himself. Jesus used Brother Sergey as an example for many things and even commented that if he became a priest, he wouldn't last too long.

"Why not?" Esteban asked.

"Too smart and too stubborn," Jesus replied.

"Too smart and too stubborn? How can you be too smart? I don't think he's stubborn at all," Esteban said.

"You'll see. It'll take time, but you'll see. In fact, he reminds me a little of Martin Luther. Sergey's also smarter than most of the teachers here. He'll grow disdainful of them. You'll see. Trust me on this." And the subject was dropped.

Students in the middle of the class knew they would be invited back as juniors. They spent the last few months alternating between loafing around and burying themselves in their studies to inch up their grade point averages. The spring and early summer days made it hard to concentrate. After all, even if they were training to be priests, they were still young men. Those at, or towards, the bottom of the class knew they weren't going to make the cut and carried on with a stiff upper lip and a resigned manner of defeat. But at least they had their self-respect and daily prayer to ask for an unexpected miracle. Esteban was among a group of gray area students who didn't know whether they'd be in or out. When not sleeping, these young men walked around with constant fear in their eyes. But, as a general rule, each dug in and worked hard.

Esteban listened in on the conversations of the elite. They spoke of taking a break and visiting family. They would get to share the pride of their families as they were introduced as Novitiates of the Gregorians. Their families would brag they had great futures as priests, monsignors, bishops, and cardinals. Graduating from the Gregorians was like graduating from Oxford or Harvard. These students were the cream of the crop and would rise to high positions within the Church. But he also listened to the hushed conversations of those who knew they would not be returning. These young men conjured a world with no tomorrow. They didn't know what they would do over the summer break or even, in fact, if they would get a break at all. They didn't know what other seminary schools would accept them as a transfer. Many talked about dropping out altogether. Maybe they weren't meant for the priesthood.

One didn't have to be a priest to be devout. Besides, there was other important work a good Catholic could conduct. Esteban despaired at these latter conversations. He made up his mind. There was no other option than to ask Brother Sergey for help.

"You want me to help you?" Brother Sergey asked.

"Very much. Everyone knows you're going to be top of the class, and I don't know who else to ask for help," Esteban said.

"Have you asked a brother or Father Peter?"

"You know I can't do that. Every time someone goes to a brother for tutorial help, it's noted and, later on, held against them."

"I'm rather busy and don't have that much spare time. In fact, I don't have any," Sergey said.

"Seriously? I need your help." Esteban was begging.

Sergey took delight in Esteban's discomfort and appeared to be mulling over the request. He was trying to find a way to use the situation to his advantage, but nothing was coming to mind.

After a moment of thought, he said, "I'll help you, but you owe me."

"Owe you what exactly?" Esteban asked.

"I don't know," Sergey replied. "But if I need a favor at some point, remember that you owe me."

"Anything, anything, I will, I will." Esteban had newfound energy and a joyful glee in his voice.

And with that, the tutorials began.

Later, after another hectic, grueling day of classes and tutoring, Esteban and Jesus walked in the warm evening Mediterranean air to get themselves a treat. Esteban got gelato, while Jesus opted for an Italian lemon ice.

On the way back, Jesus said, "Not very charitable."

"What's not charitable?" Esteban asked.

"Not what, but who," Jesus said. "Sergey. He wasn't very charitable towards you, was he? He didn't want to help you out at all."

"But he is," Esteban said in a questioning voice.

"He was more concerned about what he would get out of it. If you're not careful, payback to him could prove expensive, if not impossible," Jesus said.

"You think so?" Esteban asked.

"A word of advice, you can't trust anyone who says, 'You owe me,' before a favor is given," Jesus said in a tone demonstrating his antipathy.

Esteban heard Jesus' words, but he was tired and didn't feel like arguing.

A few weeks later, Father Peter entered the gathering hall and joined the waiting students. "Gentlemen, the school year will be over in a few short days. Our remaining time will not count towards your final grades as we'll use this time for ceremonial training. Also, we had planned to cut the bottom third, graduating only the top two-thirds of the class. However, we've been obliged to change our plans due to the demand for new priests. Therefore, we'll only cut the bottom twenty-five percent. Your grades and class position have been posted on the communal bulletin board."

Anxious murmuring and anticipation reverberated throughout the hall. Father Peter allowed the rumble to quell and resumed his announcement. "For those who didn't make the cut, please come see me at the allotted time. In some good news, the Good Lord has allowed us to find other schools if you want to pursue your priesthood."

Silence lingered in the room, and everyone listened with the utmost attention. "I'd like to take a moment to congratulate those who will be with us again next year and wish Godspeed to those who won't be back. I would also like to invite everyone to join me in congratulating Brother Sergey for finishing first."

A rapturous round of applause erupted and faded to where you could hear a pin drop.

"If there are no questions, you are all dismissed." And that was that. Father Peter turned on his heel and began to exit the hall. It was to be the last speech he would give for the year. In truth, it was the same basic speech he delivered every year. It was a speech well-practiced. In two months, his attention would again turn to the many times delivered welcoming speech. For Father Peter, a class year was divided into the speeches he gave.

Once he was out of sight, most of the novitiates rose and ran to the bulletin board. Those who knew they hadn't made the cut were in no hurry. Esteban elected to amble towards the bulletin board to find his name. He held a pit in his stomach and was not anxious to see the anticipated bad news.

"Hey, slowpoke. Why so slow?" Jesus asked.

"I'm frightened about what I'm about to learn. My gut tells me I didn't make the cut."

"You do realize that poking along isn't going to make the news any better?"

By the time Esteban arrived at the bulletin board, the crowd of brothers had thinned out. More out of reflex, he read the list from the bottom. As he reached the three-quarters mark, he felt his massive pit sink even lower into his stomach. *Have I been lucky enough to make the cut?* he wondered. But, lacking confidence, he went down to the bottom of the list to start all over again rather than continue upward.

His eyes registered his name. He wasn't in the top half of the list, but he was above the cutoff. By miracles of miracles, Esteban's name was above the line. He was in! On the way back to his room, with his spirits soaring and realizing he would be back for the third year, he stopped to contemplate why he was happy. After all, the prospect of another year like this one was not enticing.

"Why the sourpuss face?" Jesus asked.

"If they had chosen to cut where they normally would, I'd be out," Esteban said.

"So what?"

"Huh?"

"Listen, you've worked hard. You passed by the rules they set out. It makes no difference what the actual rules are. The point is, you played by those rules. Let's make no bones about it, you didn't win the race, but you finished. And for now, that's all that counts."

"You think so?" Esteban asked, brightening up a tad.

"I know so, trust me on this," Jesus said in his often-repeated phrase.

"Maybe next year won't be so hard," Esteban said with an optimistic attitude.

CHAPTER 8

CELEBRATION

"I t's nice to have you here for the summer," Uncle Pedro said. "We're so proud of you. It's a great honor to have you attend the Gregorian seminary."

"No one in our family has ever become a priest," Isabella said. Her pride was unmistakable.

"Dude, we're going to have a swell summer vacation." Jesus was laughing into Esteban's ear.

"You're spending the summer with me?" Esteban asked in a hiss, thinking Jesus was teasing.

"Wouldn't miss it for a week of veal," Jesus answered. "Besides, I've got no place to go other than the desert."

"It's a blessing. This morning, I lit two candles in prayers of thanks at church," Esteban's mother said.

Stephen Ferrari stood in the corner of the room and stared at his only child. Esteban was nineteen and stood six feet tall. Stephen admitted to himself that his son was indeed a fine-looking man, even though he was looking waned and tired. The seminary worked his son hard. Maybe being a priest wouldn't be bad for him. The Church would always look out for him. Stephen remembered his youth as a hardened chicken criminal. The thought of his time in confessionals crafting his outrageous stories caused him to crack a smile.

"Let's eat, let's eat," Isabella said. "Everything is ready."

First, there was a savory tortilla soup followed by guacamole. Next came *quesadilla de setas de temporada*, a mushroom quesadilla. The real food followed. A huge plate of Mexican veal in olive oil with zucchini and tomatoes, a chicken cacciatore, and a whole fresh Mediterranean Sea red snapper dish called *Huachinango a la Veracruzana*, graced the table. Carafes of vintage red and white wines from Tuscany helped wash down the food. Dessert was fresh fruit, cookies, and a marbled tres leches cake. There was even a sumptuous crème brûlé. The family and all their guests ate well, if not to excess. Pedro sat at the head of the table and ate with enthusiasm while beaming with pride.

During his time in Italy, fortune had been bestowed upon Pedro. His prodigious appetite was another demonstration of the power he'd attained. His two, ever-present companions consumed their food in the kitchen. Their great burps and belches reverberated into the dining room. The gastral noises bore further witness to the excellence of the meal, if not to their poor manners.

"You know, only the rich eat like this." Jesus breathed into Esteban's face, and it smelled of onions, probably from the guacamole.

After the meal, they all sat around the dining room table nibbling on nuts and marzipan. They drank carajillo, amaretto, limoncello, grappa, and Pernod. Each took turns to brag about Esteban and give thanks for the fabulous celebratory meal. They toasted his health and well-being. Embarrassed by the situation, Esteban had to sit and bear all this.

"If they knew the real truth, they wouldn't be so proud of me," he said to Jesus.

"They know the truth," Jesus said. He belched. "The truth is you're here. They're here. They've all had lots to eat and drink. They're alive, and they have hope. It has nothing to do with you. You're an excuse. So, enjoy it. I know that I am." Jesus reached past Esteban to pour another spoonful of nuts into his hand. "Excuse the reach, bud."

"What if they found out I might not make it? They wouldn't be so happy," Esteban said.

"Arrgh. You're again whining!" Jesus said. "They'd choose to feast anyway because you've made it this far. This anisette, by the way, tastes disgusting. I've got no idea why they drink this stuff. *Shreklekh!*"

All in all, that's pretty much how the whole summer went. At least once a week, there was a great meal attended by his family and friends. Every time, Esteban would receive overwhelming praise for all his accomplishments. Every boast made him feel worse and worse as he worried about his junior year in the seminary. He took frequent opportunities to unload on Jesus about how inept he felt. Jesus would try to settle Esteban by explaining that all nineteen-year-olds feel inept and that he needed to stop, "Needless complaining and whining." In lieu of whining, Jesus suggested he try to "Enjoy the food and this wonderful time with family and friends." Jesus also suggested he remind himself to "Stop and smell the roses and do this throughout the day." But, he warned, "At times, things won't always be as glorious as this summer."

In next to no time, the summer was over. The week before returning to school turned into a continuous food orgy. Esteban stayed in Rome for the whole summer and spent much of his time with Isabella. His father would come and go. Father and son didn't have many chitchats and even fewer conversations with substance. However, Esteban enjoyed many exchanges with his mother, and she always found opportunities to remind him to stay on track and follow in Jesus' ways.

"What does she know about my ways?" Jesus said to Esteban.

"She doesn't know about your terrible table manners," Esteban said.

"Right you are," Jesus said as he stuffed his mouth with a large piece of cold pizza with jalapeños, anchovies, and extra garlic.

"Say thanks and goodbye," Jesus said to Esteban at the last family gathering. "Tomorrow, we're back at school."

CHAPTER 9

SERGEY

Father Peter was on autopilot. "Today, you're starting the third year of studies to become a priest." To be honest, his mind had pivoted to a dilemma needing to be solved. His focus was on the freshmen and sophomores and finding quick replacements for five students who dropped out the day before school began.

"Let me remind you, this year won't be any easier," he heard himself saying. "In fact, some of you might find it harder because, in addition to your regular studies, you'll be expected to start setting an example for the younger men. You'll learn how to become a role model to the postulants and novices. It's not enough for a priest to give lip service to the life of our Savior." It was almost like Father Peter punctuated the period with excessive exuberance.

"We must be the personification of Christ's life. Wisdom and knowledge are nothing if not accompanied by demonstration. To think good thoughts is important. To do good deeds is even more important. To follow in the way of our Lord is the pinnacle of importance." A dramatic pause let his message sink in. He concluded his oration. "To lead the Life of Christ is your goal. As Jesus said, 'Lead, so that others may follow.'"

"Fake news! I never said that," Jesus whispered to Esteban.

"What did you say?"

"As you lead the way, be sure to help everyone sidestep the animal droppings." Jesus grinned and winked.

Esteban laughed. Jesus always had a great sense of humor and could be a real down-to-earth guy.

"Back in the day, the roads were covered with the stuff, especially from the camels. You also had sheep droppings, horse droppings, goat droppings, and dog droppings. So, when it rained, *oy gevalt*, what a mess," Jesus said. The two friends balled up in laughter until their sides hurt.

Esteban's attention was drawn back to Father Peter when he said, "We've not determined the cut for this year, but there will be one. Some of you won't make it. However, you're all encouraged to work hard. Your fate," Father Peter cupped his hand to his mouth, made a slight cough, cleared his throat, and continued. "Excuse me. As I was saying, your fate is in your own hands as much as in God's. If anyone should wish for a different room assignment, please come and see me this afternoon at two. I am delighted to announce the cooks have made special dishes for your first day back. Please be prompt for lunch and dinner. You all know the routine. Teach it to others. Brother Sergey will now lead us with a devotional service of thanks."

Father Peter smiled at the class. This was the largest class of juniors he'd ever seen, and demand for new priests was at an all-time high. Gazing around the hall, he pondered to think from where they would find new leaders. *Brother Sergey has great promise. Maybe he'll be the one to show the way. But only God knows, and he isn't telling anyone,* he thought.

Brother Sergey raised his hands and said, "Let us pray."

Good stage presence noted Father Peter and bowed his head.

That evening, Esteban said to Sergey, "I thought you did a nice job this morning." It was the first time the roommates had a chance to talk with each other all day. "How was your summer?"

"As summers go, it was okay. Poland was dreary. There isn't much to do, and there isn't the same variety of food as here. Russian operatives are always hanging around nearby, which makes everybody edgy. I can't ever see going back there to live. You think I did a good job?"

"Oh, yes. You're going to make an excellent priest. During our break, I ended up having to listen to my mother drone on and on about the Gregorians. How their priests are the elite, and they're the ones that go on to become bishops and cardinals, and sometimes even the Pope. If that's true, you're the best of the elite, and if you don't become the Pope, you'll become a cardinal."

Jesus listened to all this, stuck his tongue out, and scrunched up his face. "Not a chance," he said to Esteban, who chose to ignore him.

Sergey smiled but said nothing.

Esteban continued. "I'm delighted you're still my roommate. I wouldn't make it if I didn't have your help." This last sentence caused Sergey's ears to perk up.

"Without my help! What do you mean?" he asked with a smile disappearing from his lips and a noticeable edge to his voice.

"I thought you'd help me again this year. Like last year," Esteban replied, caught off balance by Sergey's tone.

"Oh, no, no, no. Not this year. Ain't gonna happen, sunshine! This is a new year. You'll have to pull your own weight this time, like everybody else. Don't count on me. I won't be there for you to fall back on. I've got my own problems. I can't help you. Besides, you still owe me from last year, remember?"

Esteban was crushed. Without thinking, he said, "What about what Father Peter said today about setting examples and how it was more important to do good deeds and to think good thoughts?"

"Nice one, Cyril, nice one, son. But Sergey doesn't care," Jesus said.

Sergey looked at Esteban in disbelief. "You think chubby believes any of what he says? That's the story they preach to keep idiots like you in line. That's not what this seminary is all about. The seminary is all about power and how you use it. It's about wealth and how you keep it. It's about politics and how you influence others. I'm here to deep dive into learning these things, and if you're smart, you'd take the time to learn them, too. I'm not here to help you. Besides, what would be in it for me?" Crossing his arms, Sergey gave a defiant shrug of his shoulders.

"Impressive. Very nice," Jesus said. "That's going to be hard to answer. I don't think I could answer that one."

"You agree with him?" Esteban asked Jesus in disbelief while scrunching his eyebrows.

"I never said I agreed with him. I said he made a good point. Sergey's too smart for his own good."

Fear crept into Esteban, and he began to plead. "Sergey,

you've got to help me. I won't stand a chance of making it without your help. My family wouldn't understand. My mother would be heartbroken. I'll be disgraced. Come on, you've got to help me, please?"

"Esteban, are you listening to yourself? You're whining again," Jesus said.

Sergey looked down his nose at Esteban and thought, *He has nothing I can use. He knows nothing I need to know. The best that can be said for him is that he doesn't get in my way.*

Jesus watched Sergey and said to Esteban, "Here it comes. This will be your final take-it-or-leave-it offer. Get ready."

"Okay, Esteban," Sergey said. "I'm not going to give you much time, and maybe I won't give you any. I have no real reason to help you. I have other things to do, you know."

Esteban stood there, not knowing what to say next.

Jesus broke the silence. "Looks like you're gonna be on your own there, chum. What do you have to say to the man, now?"

"I'd be grateful for any help you can give me," Esteban said meekly.

"Oh good," Jesus said. "That should make him see the light."

Sergey snorted. "I'm going for a walk. I'll see you later." He left the room.

"Well, now what do I do?" Esteban asked.

"I don't know about you, but I'm going for another lemon ice. After all, there's not too much else we can do at the moment," Jesus answered.

With classes well underway, this year was starting like no other for Esteban. He found he actually grasped what was going on. The first several weeks were spent recapping the previous year, and he used the same skills of playback that had come to his aid during the prior year. When the new material appeared, he was much better prepared than he thought. But the third month of the curricula brought back the old grind. At this time, Sergey asked some difficult questions, which put the priests on the spot. Esteban was so caught up in his own study problems he never noticed what was happening. Nevertheless, the priests noticed Sergey's questions and the tone in which he asked them. They also noticed and noted the questions' effect on the other students.

Two camps formed. One camp liked the hard, embarrassing questions and waited in awe for Sergey's next outburst. Its members enjoyed the frustration inflicted on the teachers and used it as an outlet for their own. They would discuss each priest's embarrassment and take pleasure in his hardship. The other camp thought the questions were out of place and asked out of deliberate malice. This camp felt shame and asked God to show pity on Sergey. This camp concluded that Sergey might be happier if he transferred to a different order. Sergey's lines of inquiry were all tempered with his knowledge of the unequaled need for priests and Church leaders. While they didn't care at all for his questions, nor his attitude, this camp held a grudging respect for how some of his peers looked at him.

The school year trudged on with each camp, knowing that sooner or later, the issue would have to be confronted. Neither side savored the prospect. Meanwhile, Esteban struggled on, depressed from the hard work and oblivious to what was happening all around him. Two months before the school year was to end, Sergey opened a line of questioning during a philosophy class. He wanted to know how the Church acquired and kept its wealth. The teacher had no problem with the original question. Sergey's follow-on question about wealth distribution did, however, disturb the teacher. On his part, all Sergey was trying to uncover how the money was controlled and spent, so he could get closer to it and enjoy the wealth. The teacher was having a lousy year with Sergey because the subject of philosophy can be so open to broad-ranging interpretations. During the course of the year, it had become apparent that Sergey's intellect was, in fact, superior to the teacher's. And a teacher with a bruised ego is the only thing more dangerous than a cornered feral cat. Whether intentional or not, Sergey pushed the teacher over the line and the teacher blew up. Sergey was ordered out of the class and sent to see Father Peter, where he would be disciplined. The rift had occurred.

That night, in the dorm, Sergey gloated. "They want me to apologize to the teacher and to the class."

"Why?" Esteban asked.

"Why else, so they can show they can control me." Sergey laughed.

"What are you going to do?"

"I'm going to see how popular I am," Sergey answered. "We should have the right to question our teachers, no matter how stupid we make them look. They say I must be respectful of our teachers and honor their opinions and thoughts. I'm going to see how many agree with me and how many agree with them. At a minimum, this should be fun."

Esteban had no thoughts on the subject because he was worried about a morality quiz he had to take the next day. "Sounds interesting," he said, turned off his light, and fell asleep.

The coming days saw the battle grow into a school-wide debacle. Esteban knew something was wrong, but when you're near the bottom of the class, you have to place your own needs first.

"You're behind me on this, aren't you?" Sergey asked Esteban in an aggressive and demanding manner.

"I guess so," was Esteban's reply, not sure what he was behind, but knowing he didn't want to alienate Sergey and stop what little help he could receive.

"Good, good. Thank you, Brother. I knew I could count on you."

Between classes, Father Peter noticed Esteban walking alone. "Ah, Brother Esteban, hold up. One moment of your time, please." The father walked over to him and asked, "How do you think things are going for you this year?"

"I'm trying as hard as I can," Esteban answered with a recognizable defensive tone in his voice.

"Yes, I know you're working hard. But how do you think you're doing?" Father Peter asked again. The father tended to hate these conversations.

"I guess I could do better, but I'm doing the best I can." Esteban knew he was about to be told he wouldn't make the cut. Once more, he could feel his heart sink into the pit of his stomach.

"Yes, we see that. And, how would you say Sergey is doing?" the father asked.

"I'm guessing he's doing fine."

"Do you agree with him?"

"I don't know. I don't understand. I've been too busy studying to think about it," Esteban said.

"One of the things we grade our students on is how well

they understand the Rule of the Church and the Rule of the Order. One Rule of the Order is not to question the leaders of the Order. In this case, the leaders are the teachers. The teachers are here to show the right way. Do you understand?" Father Peter asked.

"Yes, yes, I do," Esteban answered. But, in reality, he was confused and didn't grasp what he was being asked or told. Instead, his attention was being diverted to wondering what all this preamble had to do with his flunking out.

"Your grades are all passing, but only just," Father Peter said. "We haven't added in the grades for demonstration yet. You do recollect I mentioned how important demonstration was to be, don't you?"

"Oh yes," Esteban said, avaricious at an opportunity to clasp some euphoria to ease the pit in his stomach. "You said thinking good thoughts is important. Doing good deeds is even more important, and following in the way of Our Lord is the pinnacle of importance!" Esteban smiled, thinking he'd aced some type of pop quiz.

"Very good," Father Peter said. He imagined he had this one landed. "We're going to be grading soon as to how well everyone demonstrates their understanding of following the teachings of the Order. Your grades will be influenced by how well you do. A high grade means you will go on to your senior year. A low grade will mean you won't be with us next year. Do you understand me, Brother Esteban?"

"I think so," Esteban said. "Demonstration is important."

"Very good, my son," Father Peter said with a broad smile and walked away.

Sergey was coming towards Esteban from the opposite

direction and, feeling full of himself, asked, "What did chubby want?"

"To let me know I was barely passing," Esteban said.

"Anything else?"

"He told me to do good deeds and to demonstrate how well I understood the teachings of the Church."

"That's all?"

"That's all."

Jesus whispered in his ear. "You don't understand, do you?"

"Understand what?"

"What's going on. You don't understand what's going on?"

"Explain it to me," Esteban said, being a tad impatient.

"Sergey thinks it's all about how smart he can be and how he can challenge a teacher, especially since this teacher is only a brother and not a priest. He's relishing the act of ridiculing the brother. Some of the students may be enjoying it, but the priests aren't," Jesus said in a grim tone. "Sergey's failed to see that what's at issue is how well you follow the Church's leaders. To them, this is a matter of faith. You must have faith in the religion and in the Church. Sergey's actions demonstrate that you don't need to have faith. That you can keep on questioning. Well, you can't. The line had been drawn. I told you he was too smart for his own good. If he doesn't recant, he'll be expelled and may even be excommunicated."

"What should I do?" Esteban asked.

"Agree with the school. Now's not the time to make a stand and disagree. If you do, you'll find yourself somewhere else next year. A stigma will follow you, and you won't be accepted anywhere else. Now is the time for you to go along with the teachers and the priests. You need to get along. There will be another time and another place for both of us. But I can't stress enough that this is not the time." And with that, Jesus patted Esteban on the shoulder and wandered off.

Esteban looked back at Sergey and said, "You should apologize."

"What do you mean I should apologize? I'm not going to apologize. This is a matter of principle. How could you not side with me after everything I've done for you? You owed me! Remember?" Sergey was enraged. "Anyway, who told you to side with them?" he asked.

"Jesus did," Esteban answered.

By the end of the following week, Father Peter told Esteban, "You've demonstrated your understanding of our Order. Your high demonstration grade guarantees you'll make the cut this year. Who told you the right way?"

"Jesus did."

Sergey came to his senses and recanted. When word spread throughout the dorms that his roommate, Esteban, would not back him because Jesus told him not to, many felt the need to follow suit. The revolt collapsed, and all went back to worrying about their class standing.

Sergey accused Esteban of being co-opted by the school's administration. After he gave a sincere recantation and apology, Sergey asked Father Peter for a new room assignment. He also took to calling Esteban "Judas."

The priests were ecstatic at the outcome of the Sergey incident. After all, they had prevailed. Esteban had earned his high demonstration grades, especially with his now-famous answer, "Jesus did."

Esteban felt deeply wounded being called a Judas. He suffered for a period as he had liked Sergey. They had lived together for three years, and he thought of Sergey as more of an older brother than anything else.

Jesus was the only one who consoled Esteban. "Things could be worse. You could be in the desert where it's always hot," Jesus said trying to make Esteban smile. "Listen, you did the right thing. Always stay with the Church and don't take sides. You can't lose. You're gonna have to trust me on this. I'm hungry. Let's get some supper."

The school year came to a close, and the class standings were published. Sergey still finished first in the class. The school administration had not dared lower his standing for fear of giving the impression of punishing him. Father Peter now stood in front of the gathering hall and watched this large class file into the room. The Sergey incident had made for a strenuous year.

When all were seated, Father Peter began. "The third year is considered the toughest year. Next year, you'll complete your studies for the priesthood. Therefore, this will be your last summer vacation because your new assignments will begin after you graduate. I congratulate you on finishing this year and hope you all enjoy your summer. As is our custom, the student with the highest class standing will lead us in the closing ceremonies. Brother Sergey, please lead us."

Brother Sergey went to the front of the gathering hall, raised his hands, and said, "Let us pray."

Father Peter once again noted Brother Sergey's strong leadership qualities and excellent stage presence as he led the closing ceremonies. *Maybe the Jesuits would like to have him after he graduates? They're good at taking all the headache cases. Besides, the Jesuits owe us a favor!*

While Brother Esteban, aged twenty, finished almost bottom of the graduating class, he and Jesus would return for the senior year.

CHAPTER 10

OFF-KILTER

"The gelato seems fresher than usual," Esteban said.

"In all likelihood, the taste has more to do with you finishing out another year," Jesus said.

"Can you believe that! After everything that's happened, I'll be back," Esteban said while trying to imitate Arnold Schwarzenegger.

"You've applied yourself, and with free will, great things can happen."

"Free will?"

"Don't you recall that famous French thinker, Laplace, Pierre-Simon Laplace?"

"No."

"He was the one that said, '*Ce que nous connaissons est peu de chose; ce que nous ignorons est immense.*'"

"That's not helping!"

"Other than saying, 'What we know is very little; what we don't know is immense,' he also said, 'Give me the positions and velocities of all the particles in the universe, and I will predict the future.' From his way of thinking, he thought that if he could get hold of all of the data on everything that's going on at this moment, he could then use that data to predict what would happen until the end of time. But if that were true, you wouldn't be able to have free will."

"And?"

"He basically preached that everything was deterministic. At the time, that didn't sit too well with folks running in religious circles. Then, low and behold, quantum mechanics comes along, and people realize that Laplace's notion was a tad off-kilter. Not being able to predict the future is not a lack of on-hand information. There's a degree of uncertainty that's fundamental in determining determinism. You've still got one year to go before you can graduate. So, don't lose sight of all of the hard work that you'll still need to put in."

"So, you went through all of that just to tell me to work harder?"

"You and I are here for something greater. We're part of something greater, and that greatness will define our future. That's the reality, bro!"

"But what is reality?"

"Seriously?"

"Seriously."

"The first thing is to understand that reality is not just about wisdom and knowledge and what it is to be human. If reality were this empirical world and what you see, then that would just be the uppermost tip of the iceberg. There would then follow a multitude of dimensions within dimensions. There are molecules within elements, atoms within molecules, and subatomic particles within atoms. I could keep going, but we'd just end up going deeper into a rabbit hole."

"If you want to dig deeper, it's okay."

"The same thing applies to human beings. Beyond organs and limbs, within it all, under the dashboard, behind the scenes, and behind the curtain, we have ourselves and our DNA. It's the same thing with everything. Everything boils down to energy, frequency, and vibrations. You see how liquids turn into gas when heated and turn into a solid when cooled. Everything exists in a type of amorphous state, such that we can think of matter as congealed energy. And please don't get me started on quantum! How some things don't even exist until you observe them. People overrate the brain and the mind?"

Esteban was getting lost in the discourse and chose to just shrug his shoulders.

"Because if reality is beyond the mind and the mind is just one facet of reality, then the mind must therefore exist as a means to an end. So, what's the end, we can ask? To keep it all simple, we could put everything into one of two models. A physical model and a transcendent one. One essence of reality would distill things down to each individual person. Everything would then become an extension of the self and the self's needs. At that point, knowledge, information, technology, emotions, and even spirituality would merely exist to expand the needs and the horizons of the self. In other words, the center of reality would always start with you."

Jesus just received a blank look. But he was on a roll and carried on.

"Or, we could look at it the other way around and use the other model. That reality is outside of the self, and the self is just one piece of the bigger picture. To use the Hebrew words, we're talking about 'yesh' and 'ayin.' Yesh simply means an entity, something of substance, while *ayin*, means nothingness. Now, this type of nothingness is not a nothingness as in an annihilation, it's a nothingness that's a suspension of the self. Therefore, it's a state where you are not defined by who you are, but specifically, it's defined by what you are absorbing. So, absorbing that which is beyond you. And just to be clear, nothing doesn't mean nothing. It just means a different type of reality with which you're unfamiliar. You perceive nothing as nothing because you think it's invisible; you can't see it, touch it, smell it, hear it, taste it, or even think about it. So, when you're trying to get to a higher state of awareness, we're going on a journey from *yesh to ayin*."

More blank stares.

"Reality started well beyond and before your individual sense of self. So, from the top down, it began from a state of *ayin*. A state that was not defined by parameters and definitions that you have been taught. The *ayin* evolved into becoming a defined entity, namely the entity called the self. But unlike me, you have to begin at the bottom and go bottom up because you have to start with yourself. Your self-consciousness if you'd like. So, to understand reality, you'll seek something that is higher than your own self. Now, knowledge and information are important and all part of that process. It's what allows us to move from the subjective self, which gets all very emotional. Basic emotions can be distilled into I like it, I don't like it. However, if you were just an emotional creature, you'd never have an objective perspective. Every scientific theory would devolve into what's in it for me, and that could distort the theory. As you know, subjectivity, for all its value, and its value is tremendous because it's ultimately where life plays out. But on the other hand, subjective interests create prejudices and biases and involve other preconceived notions that distort an objective picture. Your mind frees you from subjectivity. But the process that you follow has to go from the bottom up, which means that you seek that which is beyond definition."

"Huh!"

"Let me continue. So, as you move from a very empirical macroscopic Newtonian picture of the universe, one that requires cause and effect, and absolutes, and determinism, you'll naturally come to discover that beneath the surface lies a quantum indeterminism. And that realization can be jolting because you'll be moving into the realm of the very subtle, and to things that aren't visible to any of your senses. And that's where reality really plays itself."

"Yes, this is all starting to become jolting! Are you done?"

"As I was saying, a more holistic view of everything would see that we're all connected. Yet, in a physical outer reality, we're not. Sergey's self-interest always conflicted with yours. Hence, there are disagreements. Some disagreements devolve to the point of divisiveness and even turn into war. Just look at history. However, when you go into the inner level, there's an intrinsic and inherent unity that connects everything. Every subatomic particle, everything is part of one larger unity. As a matter of fact, that's the reality, and everything else is an illusion. But the reality is that there's a higher reality, and you're here to discover it and channel it."

"A soulful answer, *compadre*."

"*¡Ningún problema!* We can switch topics. Have you noticed that a flame is the only physical object that defies gravity?"

"It's caused by convection," Esteban said without conviction.

"Nevertheless, in the book of Proverbs, the soul of a human being is described as being the flame of God. A flame becomes an earthly approximation to that of a soul. The point is that the soul works in the same way as a flame. It's the transcendent nature of the soul that it's always seeking to grow. In essence, it's always looking upward."

"What point are you trying to make this time?"

"Let me ask you, have you ever noticed that dead people aren't anxious?"

"That's not crossed my mind."

"Well, anxiety is the voice of your soul feeling frustrated. As the soul of a dead person has moved on, their body can't exhibit communication from the soul. All of what you've been feeling has just been your soul trying to communicate with you. Your soul is frustrated because something is out of sync."

"How can that be?"

"Ordinarily, your body normally tells you to do something via a message of pain. When it wants to eat, it sends you hunger pains; when it wants to rest, it sends you pains of fatigue; when it's worn out, it tells you your muscles ache. All of these pains are a call from your body for you to respond. It's telling you to eat a meal, drink a drink, exercise, improve your nutrition, your hygiene, and on and on."

"So."

"The soul has its own language of communication. However, its language is far more emotional and far more subliminal. Much of your angst comes from hearing your soul's different voices. Everything that you've been going through and all of the unknowns and uncertainties has definitely evoked all kinds of feelings within you. But, it's not just emotions, it's your soul speaking through your heart via your emotions. It's not something you should try and ignore by just feeling sorry for yourself. You need to know the most important part of who you are and what makes you tick."

"This has been all a bit much. Perhaps, we should see what's going on at home?"

CHAPTER 11

PRIZED POSSESSION

I sabella sighed. "You're so skinny. Aren't they feeding you?" Before he could answer, she asked him to eat. *"Come, come.* Eat, eat."

So, another summer began in the house of his Uncle Pedro with a huge meal and waves of praise for Esteban. Next year they would all be gathering at this time to celebrate his ordination as Father Esteban Ferrari. The ceremony would be held in the Vatican and afford them a lifetime of bragging rights. While he wasn't ordained just yet, nothing could prevent his mother from radiating a glow and basking in the praise of her son. It was as if she were the *objeto de deseo*. His father couldn't make the summer's opening food fest but was able to rearrange his schedule to be in Rome before the end of the following week.

Esteban had hoped to go to Frankfurt for the summer. He'd been in Rome for three years straight and wanted a break. However, his mother dismissed the idea by saying there was no city in the world like Rome, and she had closed the apartment in Frankfurt.

At the head of the table sat his Uncle Pedro, devouring a savory bowl of cioppino. His newfound love affair for Italian food had added pounds to his midriff. His power and influence had also grown. There had been an attempt on his life. The latest, was two months ago when an IED blew up his car, leaving one man dead. The dead man couldn't be identified, but rumors surfaced that he may have originated from Sardinia. Uncle Pedro's revenge reached all the way down into Italy's boot and into the port city of Palermo. A cluster of cars exploded, leaving more than a handful dead and many more wounded. The local police were puzzled. Several types of incendiary devices had been used, and some of the cars looked like they had been destroyed with advanced weaponry. Several of the dead were reputed to be key black marketeers. After the deaths, more rumors circulated. Word on the street was that a meeting took place in Sorrento. An unidentified go-between transferred large sums of money to extend Pedro's protection to those who had dealings with Palermo's recently deceased. Pedro adopted the attitude that if you can't beat them, join them, regardless of the cost. After all that, and at least for the time being, things were peaceful again.

Back at the meal, Jesus was elated. Between mouthfuls, he spluttered to Esteban. "Yummy. Get ready for this season's food debauchery. Pass the linguini, *amico*."

Like Pedro, Jesus was starting to develop a serious hankering for Italian food. This summer was a rerun of last summer's events. As the warm Mediterranean climate wore on, Esteban complained to Jesus about how tiresome the summer had become. He was anxious to return to school.

"You are always anxious to be someplace else," Jesus said dryly. "But you know what? I was the same way. At twenty, I also wanted to be someplace else. Thinking back, I remember it was to be anyplace else. If I had to saw one more board of acacia, or if I was asked to make one more door or shutter, or to smooth finish one more chair, I would literally puke. If only I had known what I know now. I had the touch, they said. I was married to the wood, they said. If they only knew how true that would turn out to be! I'd like another helping of steak pizzaiola. More sauce and a big chunk of that bread. *Grazie, grazie.*"

"Your table manners could still use a fair amount of improvement. Didn't you ever learn any?" Esteban asked while serving up the food.

"We didn't have forks or knives when I was a kid. Only spoons. More mostaccioli, guv," Jesus said.

"What do you mean you didn't have knives and forks? What kind of excuse is that for your poor manners?" Esteban asked, spooning the pasta onto Jesus' dish.

"An honest one." Jesus belched. "I don't know if I want more pasta or a cannoli. Your problem is you don't know anything about history. When you studied Marco Polo, you were taught how he took Christianity to the heathen Mongols and brought back great riches. His discoveries were supposed to have opened trade with the East. That's not the way it went down. Oh, that lasagna looks so good. Your mama learned how to make a mean lasagna. Give me some of that." Jesus sat and chewed the lasagna with a contented look on his face.

"Marco Polo! What's that got to do with knives and forks?" Esteban asked.

"What? Oh," Jesus said, and he returned to his story. "The

real treasures he brought back were not the jewels he happened to sew into his robes, but things considered worthless and carried in plain sight. For example, he brought back the tomato and the recipe for turning flour into noodles. The Mongols loved noodles and took great pride in how they were made. Tomatoes were eaten raw, stir-fried, and even pickled. A true delicacy. Together, these were all symbols of long life and happiness." At that point, Jesus noticed an uncut cherry tomato on the table and popped that into his mouth. He resumed—his words coming out a tad muddled until he finished swallowing—"But they had trouble eating the long noodles with chopsticks, so they invented the fork, which they decided was too clumsy to use with anything else. Those were the real treasures. The instruments changed life in Italy, and much of Europe and the rest of the world fell under early Italian and Spanish influence. Furthermore, since I lived well before Marco Polo's time, I hadn't encountered a fork until we met. I'm stuffed. I don't think I can eat another cannoli. Maybe, if I forced myself." Jesus passed gas. "Oops." He giggled.

"What an outright pig!" Esteban said. "That's it? That's your story? You expect me to believe that? You made it up! Didn't you?"

"I'm Jesus. I don't make anything up. There's one more thing I forgot to mention. Marco Polo also brought back something else that manifested in a lot of changes."

"This should be good, and what was that?"

"The Great Khan was so impressed with Christianity that he gave Polo a toy used to light up the sky at night. The Mongols loved fireworks, and they called the powder a heavenly light. For whatever reason, Genghis lost interest in me and took up the teachings of my distant cousin, Buddha. He felt my teachings weren't peaceful enough. He had the last laugh, though."

"How was that?" Esteban asked.

"The Mongols used the powder to light the night skies and to bring them happiness. The Italians changed the name from heavenly light to gunpowder and used it to bring them happiness by killing other men. What irks me about all this is that most of the killing was claimed to be done in my name, and for my sake. They never asked me how I felt about it! The barbarian Mongols gave the civilized white man a way to feed himself and a way to kill himself. The Mongols call this yin and yang. I call it outright bonkers! Give me an apple. I've noticed I don't get any smarter when I eat these. How 'bout you?"

As the weeks wore on and Esteban found the summer tiresome. His mother was overbearing and ever more prideful. Esteban translated her reveling into feeling intense pressure, and he felt terrible. To make matters worse, Jesus teased him all the time about her. Every time Isabella said, "And this is my son, Esteban, the priest," he'd correct her with, "Not until next year, Mama." Jesus would laugh and laugh and say, "Not bad, not bad, not too shabby at all."

"Not bad. It's terrible," Esteban said.

"Oh, I don't know," Jesus said. "My mother never introduced me as 'my son, the carpenter.' And she never ever introduced me as 'my son, the Son of God,' at least not when Yosef was around. It could be worse. Strike that, it will be worse. You'll see. It was for me, anyway. When I went to live with the Essenes, I often wished my mother was there to make me a nice cholent or to bake me some matzah, as only she could. I would've been happy for any introduction from my mother, so stop complaining."

"What do you know?" Esteban asked.

"I'm Jesus, and I know everything. It comes with the territory. And if, for some reason, I don't, my father does."

With a few days to go before school was set to begin, Stephen showed up. He hadn't been around much, and on the few occasions he was in Rome, he'd been preoccupied and too busy to offer any real attention. After dinner, Esteban was invited to join him and Pedro in the study. Such an invitation had not previously been extended to Esteban. Pedro's study was off limits and kept under lock and key.

"Sit here," Uncle Pedro said in a warm tone as he sat behind his colossal wooden desk with its dark mahogany wood polished to a glaring shine.

"Very nice wood. The carpentry's excellent. You can see it's all been hand-finished," Jesus said.

Esteban sat in an oversized, oxblood-colored leather chair. His father sat next to him in a matching piece of furniture. Pedro's two ever-present associates busied themselves by pouring Sambucas, and handing out large Cuban cigars. Jesus sat in a chair behind Esteban and his dad.

"*Salud*," Pedro said.

"*Salud*," the other men said.

The ritual format was new to Esteban, but he raised his glass to imitate the others. Pedro and Stephen smiled and once again raised their glasses to Esteban. They all tilted their heads back and drained their pony glasses. Esteban did likewise and almost gasped at the intense flavor and coughed from the strong burn as he swallowed. His eyes teared. He was thankful no one was paying any attention to his discomfort except Jesus, who wheezed while saying, "Good stuff, huh?"

"How's school?" his father asked.

"Fine. School is good."

"Do you have any idea where they will send you when you become a priest?"

"No, not yet," Esteban replied, afraid this was going to turn into the Spanish Inquisition. The last person who opened up a conversation with Esteban by asking how he was doing was Father Peter. That conversation ended up causing him considerable consternation regarding his friend Sergey. However, his fears that the questioning would continue were unwarranted as neither his father nor uncle pursued the issue.

The room fell silent. Pedro motioned to his men, and more Sambuca was poured.

"I don't think I could drink another," Jesus said.

"Esteban, you remember when you found out Signore Romero died?" Uncle Pedro asked.

"Yes, he might have done something illegal," Esteban answered.

"That's not true, those bastards," Stephen said. "Romero was a fine man. An honorable man. A man of business and principle.

"He was too damn smart," Pedro said in support of Stephen, and raising his glass, he said, "To the Signore, *salud*!"

"*Salud*!" The glasses were refilled.

"He was most fond of you, Esteban," Stephen said. "The Signore had no family of his own and considered you as a son."

"I liked him," Esteban said. "I cried when I read online about his death."

"Esteban, the Signore left you what he considered his most valuable possession. This is the key that opens that heavy trunk. The privilege of opening belongs only to you," Stephen said as he placed the key in Esteban's palm.

It took both of Pedro's goliaths to pick up the trunk and place it in front of Esteban.

"I love surprises," Jesus said, clapping. "This is way cooler than trying to bite into an apple placed in a bucket of water during Purim. Come on, hurry up, and open it."

Smiling, Esteban placed the key in the lock and turned. The clasp fell away, and he unlatched the closures. He pushed back on the Brazilian cherry wood top, which raised smoothly on its well-oiled hinges.

"Books. It's full of books." Esteban beamed in surprise.

"Only books?" Pedro asked from behind his colossal wooden desk.

"Just books," Stephen answered.

Pedro looked at his associates. "Check through the books."

Every book in the chest was taken out, and the pages were painstakingly leafed.

One of the men grunted. "Nothing but books."

Stephen and Pedro had both expected to uncover something of monetary significance. Disappointed, Pedro said, "Put the books away." The big men complied.

"Esteban, I hope you relish reading these books. Signore Romero always talked about how much he enjoyed reading Don Something or Other with you. He told me you'll also enjoy reading the other books. Keep them safe. Do that as an honor to the Signore, a true resourceful gentleman," said Stephen.

"A businessman, a man of honor and principle," said Pedro. The glasses were filled one more time.

"*Salud,*" this time, said in unison.

The books were a joy to Esteban. He reread *Don Something or Other* and recalled, with joy, the time he and the Signore read together. The books had become the treasure the Signore had hoped, his most valued possessions. Jesus laughed and mentioned that if it were him, he'd prefer a week of veal and a month of pizza.

During the last couple of days before school, Esteban felt his father wanted to tell him something but never quite got around to it. However, he did give Esteban a note from the Signore that read, "My dearest Esteban, please take the time to read my old books. Things may not always be as they seem. Think about it. Warmest regards." It was signed, Signore Romero.

The night before the first day of school, the summer was over with the serving of the last great meal. Mother was proud. Esteban had gained ten pounds from her forced feeding. Jesus ate with great relish and consumed everything in sight.

"It'll never be like this again." He burped. "It's time to say so long, and thanks for all the fish."

CHAPTER 12

FINAL YEAR

"Greetings, good morning, fathers, may the Lord be with you," Father Peter said. There was a burst of low nervous laughter from the returning seniors. "Before you become fathers, you must complete your final year of training and preparation. We'll address you with your pending title. That way, you can feel the responsibility and gravity that comes with being a priest. This year will not be any easier. It might even be harder. You'll begin to spend time with local churches helping their priests. Of course, you'll be expected to keep up with your studies." Father Peter let the message to the students sink in. "You'll all have individual cells. No roommates this year. No doubt that will please the multitude! From here on out, you'll live like a priest, think like a priest, act like a priest, and be treated like a priest. Are there any questions?"

Father Peter was in a quandary. He didn't know how the abbot would explain to the Pope that so many students decided not to return for their final year. The Pope wasn't going to be a happy camper. *I'm glad it's not my problem,* he thought. "As there are no further questions, Father Sergey, please lead us in a short prayer of thanks."

Esteban noticed Sergey had gained a further air of authority, a certain *je ne sais quoi* presence about him. A person who knew what he was about and why. Father Peter also noticed and prayed in silence this coming year would not be a repeat of the last. *He has the potential. He has the potential!* he kept reiterating in his head.

"Let us pray," Father Sergey said.

Majestic. What presence, Father Peter thought again.

The class filed out of the chapel. The kickoff for the final year had begun in earnest. Esteban was the last to leave. Father Peter noticed Esteban leaving and thought, *I hope he makes it. He's always last. Not like Sergey, who's always first.*

The first two months were spent reviewing last year's material, and Esteban handled the pressure without major distress. At times, he found it isolating to have his own room but managed to adjust. Jesus was always nearby whenever he ran into an issue, which was nice. He got a real kick out of working with the priests at the local churches. The work tended to be running small errands, but it allowed Esteban to roam around the streets of Rome and act all high and mighty. He was enjoying being treated like a real priest. Jesus chided him for not taking the work seriously and looking upon the tasks as a way of staying out of the classroom. Esteban disagreed as the best part was not being stuck in a classroom. When he stopped at a ristorante to get a meal or a cup of coffee, the waitpersons would treat him with deference and accept his blessing in lieu of a tip. Convenient for a young priest strapped for cash.

On Sundays, he was allowed to help serve Mass, a task he considered play. A feeling carried over from when he was little more than a senior altar boy. Some priests did all the work and took all the joy out of the service for those assigned to help. A few of the older priests went through the motions, having long since forgotten or cared about what they were doing. A job is a job, and in their job, Sunday was the intensive workday of the week. Some of the sermons Esteban heard were inspiring, and others almost put him to sleep. From time to time, Esteban heard confessions.

The seasoned priests tended to put on their most serious faces whenever they listened to their parishioners' innermost secrets and fears. Some priests laughed after the sinner left the confessional and mocked the paltry sins they heard. Some priests would clammer for the good old days when people committed grave and meaty sins. Too many of the modern-day sins were mundane. To Esteban, this was all quite serious. He fretted about whether he could learn to give proper penance. He was instructed not to worry, that whatever penance he decided would be accepted with pride by the sinner. He was also informed how some sinners would use severe penance as a bragging right. Listening to confession was an eye-opening experience for Esteban. He was surprised about the commonality of certain sins and how many sought forgiveness for having an impure thought. He found this all beguiling as listening to a confession about having an impure thought caused him, in turn, also to have an impure thought. On this topic, Esteban sought counsel.

"Father, when you listen to a confession of lust, what do you think about?" Esteban asked.

"Nothing," the priest replied.

"Nothing?"

"Nothing."

"That's good advice," Jesus said.

"I'm confused," Esteban said.

"You're supposed to be," Jesus said. "What do you think the real job of a priest entails? Don't answer, I'll tell you."

Jesus motioned Esteban to one side. "A priest acts as a message carrier between the repentant and God. He passes judgment and offers forgiveness at the same time by giving penance. The priests who think they are the most forgiving are the ones who pass out the hardest penance. It's easy. You listen, you forgive. Step one, step two. Listen, then forgive. It's easy."

"Oh, okay," Esteban said.

When the classroom work became befuddling, he gave his all and tried hard. He became adept at playing back what was taught to him. Many teaching priests noted this and were inclined to give him a break on their grading. These priests were further encouraged to help him because of the urging of the abbot to make sure as many of the class as possible would graduate. The Holy Father was banking on the Gregorians to provide new priests.

The time away from the school gave Esteban a chance to be out from under the watchful eyes of the seminary. He pointed this out to Jesus.

"Playing priest and visiting these churches is a pretty nice gig," he said to Jesus.

"How's that?" Jesus asked.

"I'm away from my teachers and the other observers' eyes, which is helping me to pass. Besides, it also keeps me from worrying," Esteban answered.

"Worrying wouldn't help you anyway, and I understand why you would want to stay hidden. I felt the same way at one point," Jesus said.

"You did? When was that?" Esteban asked. "I don't believe you."

"How many times do I have to tell you? I'm Jesus, and I'm always going to speak the truth. I tried to hide out twice, in fact. Once when I was eighteen and again when I was twenty-five. Much to my chagrin, things didn't work out either time."

"How come? And since you're Jesus, why did you hide out, and where did you hide out?"

"You're asking a lot of questions, young man. Is there anything else you'd like to know while you're at it?" Jesus asked.

"Not for now."

"Good. Here's how it all went down. I was about to turn eighteen, and my teacher in the Essenes, Rabbi Moshe, told me the leaders wanted me to become a teacher. He told me I had some unearthly ability to explain things and that I was wise beyond my years. But we have to put this in perspective. You need to recognize my lineage, and from whom I inherited my intelligence. The invitation to become a teacher was a great honor. It was also a great responsibility. At the time, I didn't want to do it. Rabbi Moshe even raised his voice when I told him I didn't want to become a teacher. He told me I had a moral and ethical responsibility to teach others what I knew. Essene leaders never raise their voices. So, this was all unusual. I held my ground and refused to obey. They put a lot of pressure on me to comply, so I chose to run away. I felt I had won that round and was gone for more than a year."

"Where did you go?" Esteban asked, positive his friend was about to contrive another fanciful shaggy dog story.

"Where I was sure they'd never look for me, in the desert. They knew I had a disdain for the hard desert life, so they looked for me in the towns and cities. I fooled them. I thought I outsmarted the whole bunch of them. But it turned out I was miserable out there. It took me the better part of a year to figure out I was on the short end of the stick. I was being put out, not my teachers. Finally, they tracked me down, and I went back. I was humiliated, but I went back."

"How were they able to find you?"

"By accident, of course. I was pretty good at some magic tricks, and between my carpentry work and performing tricks, I could scrape together a meager living. Enough to get by, at least. The nomads thought I was funny, and word got out about me across the different watering holes. My fame had already begun. That's how the Essenes got wind of my whereabouts. To this day, I'm surprised by their approach. They didn't threaten me and asked if I was ready to return. Instead, they told me if I didn't want to teach, that was okay. The desert is a tough place to live. I missed out on all the good things by hiding, and it turned out, I wasn't being overlooked or forgotten. They knew sooner or later, I'd be back."

"What happened when you returned?" Esteban asked.

"Nothing. They all acted like I never went away. And, without additional pressure, I learned how to teach and what to teach."

"What about the second time you hid? Where were you?"

"In the cities. I hid there for five years, right under the noses of the authorities. It turns out the easiest place to hide is always in plain sight. This is a great story. You'll love this one.

Simon said I preached for three years, it was actually eight. Simon only knew me for three years, and he took it for granted I only taught for the time he knew me. That's not what happened. I left the desert when I was twenty-five and was hired to teach children how to read. Their parents soon began attending my classes because they didn't know how to read either. One thing led to another, and I began commenting on how they led their lives. I echoed all the things Rabbi Moshe had taught me but in my own inimitable style. It didn't make me popular with the authorities, but the people lapped it up! They couldn't get enough. The critics, the ones in charge, knew I was once an Essene, so they looked for me in the desert. By the time I was thirty, people knew of me everywhere I went. For three years, I was famous, which made the Romans unhappy, but you already know how the story turns out."

Esteban was quiet for a few moments before asking, "Why did you tell me all this?"

"I was explaining what I learned about hiding," Jesus answered.

"To be honest, I missed your point," Esteban said.

"I'm not surprised. I learned I missed the bad when I hid but also the good. It happens that way."

"I'll take my chances." Esteban laughed.

"Don't you always!" Jesus laughed as well.

The year went on. Esteban didn't see much of his classmates after school. Sergey was establishing his fan club. And, he still had the occasional run-in with the faculty. Still, it became apparent to most that he would have to be assigned to an order that could tolerate his intellectual idiosyncrasies. By the year's midpoint, the senior-year priests began wondering about their upcoming assignments. Rumors began to fly about what kind of work each would do and where. One rumor had the top ten assigned to work in the Vatican. The rumor wasn't true, but Father Peter didn't squash it as it helped stimulate competition.

"You don't get good rumors like that crop up every day," he said to the abbot, who agreed. The abbot and his staff had already begun furnishing a special committee established on behalf of the Pope with profiles of the young men. The committee would be charged with deciding who would go where and why. Their selection and review criteria were top secret. But as with most professional matters, the criteria became political. With all the talk at the seminary, Esteban remained oblivious to anything the rumor mill was churning out. He was hoping he had done enough to graduate. Out of nowhere, something happened to make him forget all about school.

His father disappeared.

He learned of the matter as he entered Pedro's apartment for Friday evening supper after finishing helping a priest at a nearby church during the day. "What do you mean, he's disappeared?" he heard his mother ask of her brother.

"He wasn't on the afternoon flight from Berlin," Pedro answered.

"Where is he?" Isabella asked.

"I have no idea."

"What do you mean? You always know where he is and what he's doing."

"Isabella," Pedro said in a stern voice. "I'm only a business associate. I'm not his keeper. You're being disrespectful, and I won't tolerate it. If I knew where he was, I'd tell you. He missed his flight and will catch the next one."

Isabella calmed the tenor of her voice. "I've never known him not to show up. He'll always call or text. Something's wrong."

"Nothing is wrong," Pedro said, noting the change in Isabella's manner. "He'll be home by tomorrow."

Dinner was subdued, and not even Uncle Pedro ate with any enthusiasm. Only Jesus didn't let the tension bother him. He had his usual appetite and ate like there was no tomorrow. Esteban couldn't believe his eyes. Jesus downed two bowls of soup and ripped through the antipasto like he was afraid he'd miss out on an after-Christmas sale at Harrods. The shrimp scampi never had a chance. Jesus rushed in to sop up the rich garlic butter with the oven-fresh warm crusty bread. The gnocchi in a spicy marinara sauce with sausage was inhaled, and the veal with sweet and hot peppers were demolished in no time.

"How can you eat like that at a time like this?" Esteban wanted to know.

"Worry makes me hungry," Jesus answered. "Besides, you should never let anything interfere with a great supper. You never know when it's going to be your last."

Several of Uncle Pedro's business associates stopped by during the meal. Each time, he got up from the table and walked to his study to spend a few minutes away from the family. Upon returning, he would say, "Don't worry. It wasn't anything to do with Stephen." In turn, everyone believed it had something to do with him, but nobody dared to challenge the statement. Midnight rolled around, and there was still no word. Everyone spent a sleepless night in anticipation of bad news. Early Saturday morning, Esteban went off to help at a nearby church. As he left, he told his mother not to worry.

She replied with a wry smile. "He always warned me, one day, he wouldn't bother to come home."

Stephen Ferrari was never found. Seven years later, he would be declared legally dead. Many theories surfaced as to his disappearance. Some speculated he was a reprisal victim against Pedro. Some speculated Stephen had greased the wrong palms. Others said his business had taken a sour turn, and he was to blame. A few cynical people said he had all he could of Isabella and had taken off with a more loving younger woman. The police researched every story and tried to connect every loose end, but no evidence cropped up to corroborate any of the theories. After ninety days, they gave up. Isabella blamed everyone and loudly claimed Stephen wouldn't just leave her. Not after more than twenty years of marriage.

Over time, she continued to struggle with Stephen's disappearance. She wanted to believe she could uncover a switch to turn off the guilt of not knowing what happened. Sometimes, in life, there are no answers. But, at least, she could find solace in her Esteban.

The disappearance of his father had an adverse effect on Esteban's immediate schoolwork. Jesus tried to encourage him to get on with it, but Esteban developed a funk that couldn't and wouldn't budge.

"It's all my fault that he's gone," Esteban said.

"How's that?" Jesus asked.

"He never wanted me to become a priest. He left so he wouldn't have to see me ordained."

"Where on earth did you come up with that crazy idea?"

"My mother always told me not to listen to him. He wasn't a good Catholic. She told me he would sooner die than see me become a priest. It's all my fault."

"Your mother made that all up. He never said any such thing. On the contrary, he was proud of you. Your mother said those things because she feels guilty about his disappearance and is trying to lay blame elsewhere. Your father not returning has nothing to do with your becoming a priest," Jesus said.

"How do you know that?" Esteban said.

"I'm Jesus."

"And, you know everything?"

Jesus smiled and nodded.

At school, Esteban's teachers were divided on what to do about him. Half suggested his father's disappearance had a harmful effect on his grades and should be excused because of the emotional impact. The other half held forth that he was never a great student outside of languages, of which he was now fluent in English, Italian, Spanish, German, Bavarian, French, Latin, Greek, Polish, Aramaic, and Hebrew, and should be afforded no special easement of the requirements. They further counseled by saying a priest often had to perform duties during moments of duress. That many priests would encounter troubling times from which they would need to find the strength to cope. Therefore, he should be judged on an equal footing with every other student.

In the end, it became a moot point. During the last month of school, Esteban passed all his finals. He had found a higher force to pull himself up by the bootstraps, pushed aside his funk, and put in a lot of hard work. Jesus' constant cajoling helped too. Inspiration, or a guilt trip, also came from his mother. She reminded him that she would die alone and heartbroken if he didn't become a priest.

CHAPTER 13

MINOR ADJUSTMENT

The abbot sent a letter to the Committee for Priest Placement stating the graduating class would be ordained on the first Sunday in June. They would all accept the calling and were ready to be assigned wherever the Lord and the Church deemed appropriate. The committee took its function to heart and reported to the Pope. They were responsible for matching each candidate with an acceptable assignment. Considering the political intrigue, it was not a casual task.

"Our first candidate is Father Sergey. You all know Father Sergey. Where should we send him?" the leader of the committee asked.

Each member sitting at the long table knew firsthand about him. The members represented one or more of the key orders or organizations of the Church and were there to protect specific interests. Moreover, each knew Sergey's reputation for great intellect and remarkable debating skills. The members eased the tension of their debating by joking about how he could argue the difference between day and night, and after he had convinced you of his point of view, switch sides to keep the discussion going. Nobody liked to debate matters of faith or policy with Sergey. On the issue of Church wealth, discussions with him were avoided at all costs. The table was quiet as each member weighed the consequences of taking on his intellect and dealing with his challenging attitude. He was the quintessential loose cannon.

The committee leader spoke up again. "Where shall we send him?"

"The North Pole," a meek voice in the room answered. Everyone laughed.

"Good idea," the leader said. "It's too bad we don't have a chapel there. But cut me some slack and help me on this one. Where shall we send him?"

The room fell silent. A few moments passed, and the quiet voice spoke up again. "Why not send him to Las Cruces?"

Once again, everyone laughed. That particular assignment had been open for the past three years. Las Cruces was a small, dusty, dry farming town in Central Mexico where the land was more desert than arable. Its small population tended to be more indigenous than Mexican. The residents who were Catholic also practiced a bizarre brand of the faith.

Las Cruces had been on their list for a long time but nobody wanted to accept the assignment. The last two priests the committee had assigned ended up leaving the priesthood altogether. One resigned his vows after being seduced by the sensuous women and the general attitude of *mañana* that prevailed throughout the town. The other found the allure of the primitive customs irresistible, including the strong hallucinogenic drugs the indigenous Indians brewed. The story said that the drugs fried the priest's brain.

Each committee member was familiar with the horror stories associated with Las Cruces. Even though the assignment had been open for the last three years, the parish hadn't had any clergy for far longer. The last long-term priest had gone senile. One day, he decided to walk into the desert during the hottest part of the day, and was never seen again. The Indians said he was eaten by the giant sun snake that preyed on anything that moved during the hot, sun-drenched hot afternoons. A search party was organized, but no one found the slightest trace.

The Cardinal of Mexico had been unable to recruit anyone from his own ranks due to the acute shortage of priests and the unpopularity of the location. The Cardinal was forced to appeal to the Pontiff for help. The Pontiff delegated the responsibility to the committee. The Cardinal of Mexico was applying pressure on the Holy See for a new priest by reducing the amount of money he sent to Rome. The situation had become a matter of principle for the Cardinal of Mexico. The Pope had not delivered on his promise, so the cardinal slowed the revenue stream further. This year, no matter what, the post had to be filled. Not only would the Pope send a new priest, but he also would send a Gregorian graduate. An elite priest was destined to grace Las Cruces.

The committee member who had made the suggestion waited for the laughter to stop. "Think about it. We'd solve two problems at one time. We all know Father Sergey is brilliant, but shall we say, he has some bothersome traits. Several years in the desert might help him see the light and our way of thinking." He let the room digest the thought. "If he concludes wealth is wrong, let him serve those living in poverty. He'll be happy to return to us in two or three years. The Pope will be able to report to the Cardinal of Mexico that he is sending our number one graduate. The cardinal will be obligated to increase his contributions and give his full support to His Holiness on many other pressing issues."

The members contemplated the clarity and wisdom of the argument. Within minutes, the silence was broken. The members were of like minds, and each voiced agreement. The committee head said he'd have His Holiness informed right away.

"Who's next?" the head member asked.

Word was sent to the Pope, and the committee continued doling out assignments. It had finished all but a few assignments in less than three days, including the required paperwork. The new priests would receive their assignments on the Monday following their ordinations. The last handful of assignments lived up to the rule of thumb: the least important things take the longest to perform. In the afternoon, at three minutes past three, the committee got ready to discuss Father Esteban Ferrari.

"He isn't exactly the brightest bulb on the Christmas tree," one member said while reviewing Esteban's record.

"Not by a long shot," another said.

Someone else said, "But, he's a very pious young man and does as he's asked."

"In his third year, he was the first man to side with the school administration when Father Sergey initiated his rebellion. His action broke a tense situation. As already pointed out, he may not be the brightest, but he is one of us."

The committee head said, "We have an unimportant

opening. We need a priest to assist the Head of Protocol. His duties wouldn't amount to anything more than serving as an errand boy. The work is easy, and because it's here in the Vatican, the position has some prestige. He's perfect."

The committee was growing tired, and everyone wanted to finish, so they reached an agreement on the spot. All the new priests had been assigned, and the committee members were free to attend to their regular duties. They held a banquet with the staff from the Gregorian seminary to celebrate a successful year. The Pope would be delighted with the decisions.

But things do not always work out as hoped. On the Saturday before the ordination ceremony, the committee head and the abbot received a summons to the office of one of the secretaries to the Pope in the Vatican.

"I've finished reviewing all the appointments for this year's graduates and reviewed them with His Holiness," the secretary said.

The two men were not offered coffee or any type of refreshment, a clue the meeting was to be short.

"For the most part, His Holiness has no problem with any of the assignments and believes you've done an admirable job."

The two men smiled at the praise and said, "*Gratias tibi,* thank you."

"He thinks you might have misunderstood the importance of the Assistant to the Head of Protocol assignment. His Holiness wishes to stress the importance of this position. In these trying times, this particular priest might end up being a spokesman for His Holiness. He wonders if you might be able to change an assignment or two to find somebody he feels is more suitable."

The two men understood the exact nature of what was being asked.

"Who do you think might be more acceptable to His Holiness?" the committee head asked.

"The Pontiff wishes to have the top graduate placed in that assignment," answered the secretary in a nonchalant manner.

"That would be Father Sergey," the abbot said.

"The top graduate?" the secretary asked.

"Yes, he is."

They realized the secretary's comment was rhetorical. After a few seconds of uncomfortable silence, the secretary said, "May I ask you to step into the next office and ponder the assignment list? I'm sure you'll be able to conclude everything in no time."

Both men scanned the lists in the adjoining office, trying to figure out who to change with Father Sergey and Father Esteban. "This is hard," the abbot said. He had not been privy to the committee's assignment criteria.

The committee head picked up the telephone and, after the usual preliminaries, said, "Has all the assignment paperwork been completed?"

He placed his hand over the mouthpiece as he listened and said to the abbot, "Let's make this easy."

The abbot nodded his head in agreement.

The committee head said, "I understand what you are saying, but we must make a minor change. Please exchange the assignments for Father Sergey and Father Esteban. Yes, that's right. Father Sergey will stay in Rome, and Father Esteban will go to Mexico. Redo their paperwork with the utmost haste. Make this your number one priority, and have everything ready by the time I get back. Thank you. *Ciao*."

Smiling, the two men reentered the secretary's office, and the abbot said, "Everything has been addressed. *Audeat est facere,* to dare is to do. Father Sergey will remain here in Rome."

"Oh, good. The Pontiff will be so delighted," the secretary said.

CHAPTER 14

ORDINATION

The Sacrament of Ordination is a significant ceremony. The ceremony is celebrated in conjunction with a High Mass. Translated, the ritual takes a long time. The rite traces back to the Last Supper when Christ conferred on man the power of consecrating and offering the body and blood of Christ and of remitting and retaining sins.

The Pope chose to preside over the service. This was a large class of Gregorians, in all probability the future leaders of the Church. The Pope's participation made a grand spectacle even more extravagant. Only at Easter and Christmas would more finery be on display. The most beautiful linens and accoutrements were displayed. The attendants to the Mass, the priests, altar boys, choir, and musicians, were all majestic in their vestments. The Pope performed the laying on of hands, placing his hands on the head of each young man and sharing a few moments of silent prayer. It was an inspiring moment for each ordained father.

Esteban's beaming mother and uncle attended the ceremony. Esteban looked around the church during the ceremony and noticed the sheer size of the audience. It took a long time for him to locate his mother. Isabella told him she would wear a large black hat so she would stand out. However, every other mother in attendance had adopted the same game plan. When the Pope got to Esteban, he placed his hands on his head. Seconds later, he moved on to the next man. Esteban could swear he heard his mother swoon with joy. After the Pope finished, he returned to the center of the altar. He broke the long silence by saying, "We ask you, all-powerful Father, give these servants of yours the dignity of the Presbyterate. Renew the Spirit of holiness within them. By your divine gift, may they attain the second order in the hierarchy and exemplify right conduct in their lives."

And with those words, Esteban Ferrari became a priest of the Holy Roman Catholic Church. He had become a Priest of the Faithful; he had crossed the finishing line.

After the ceremony, the majority of attending families threw spectacular parties. All over Rome, people were celebrating. Open houses lasted until the early hours of the morning. People traversed the city, going from one home to the next to congratulate the new priests and their respective families and to share a glass of wine and a bite to eat. Isabella and Pedro hosted a magnificent open house. The food poured out of the kitchen all afternoon and all night. Whoever stopped by the house to visit was greeted with "*Mangiare, mangiare.*" Everyone wished Father Esteban Ferrari well.

Jesus was in his element. Whatever was on the table hit his plate, and not in tiny portions. He was out eating Uncle Pedro and his two lieutenants combined.

"Why are you eating like that?" Esteban asked Jesus.

"Why do you need to know?"

Esteban had no response.

Father Esteban met more people than he imagined existed. Friends had friends who had friends who had friends, and all showed up to shake his hand and enjoy the food and libations. The house was full of people, and full of food, wine, and good cheer. And much to Esteban's surprise, his father was never mentioned. Not by anyone, not even once.

"This is way better than Christmas," Jesus said as he ate another helping of fritto misto. Jesus always burped when he was speed eating, and tonight, he was out doing his own low standards. Esteban tried his question again.

"Why are you eating like this?"

"Fattening the Paschal Lamb," was the answer delivered mid-burp.

"What's that supposed to mean?"

"Chill, Esteban. You've graduated. School is out. There may be lean times ahead. I want to be ready. I've already told you about how they tried to make me a teacher when I graduated. Be prepared in case of lean times. I'm fattening up now."

"Well, haven't you heard, I'm getting a good assignment, so there's no need to be so piggish," Esteban said.

"I hadn't heard. How do you know?" Jesus asked.

"Well, that's the rumor going around. I'm going to be staying here in Rome, at the Vatican," was the smug reply.

"Oh, is that a true fact?" Jesus asked.

"Yes, it is. One of my classmates overheard two members of the assignment committee talking about it." This reply from Esteban was even smugger.

Jesus laughed, belched, and helped himself to the antipasto, two lamb chops, and a nice large piece of crusty fresh bread. "The only thing better than lamb chops is veal chops," he said as he poured himself a glass of Chianti. He raised his glass and toasted Esteban. "Here's to no lean times or rumors of its non-existence."

Before Esteban could ask Jesus what was meant by the remark, he was interrupted and introduced to another visitor, a beautiful nineteen-year-old woman.

They stood and made some small talk. Out of nowhere, the girl said, "Will you hear my confession?" At first, Esteban didn't know what to say.

Jesus said to him, "Father Esteban Ferrari is who you are now. You'll often hear that question."

"Should I hear her confession?" Esteban asked.

"Of course. It's your job, and it's why you're a priest," Jesus answered.

"But we're not in a church," Esteban said, afraid of the responsibility.

"You know that makes no difference," Jesus said with a great deal of impatience. "Go find a nice quiet place and hear this fine young lady's confession."

"Of course, I'll hear your confession. That's what a priest does, even a new priest," Father Esteban said. "Let's see if we can find somewhere quiet for a few minutes."

As it turned out, the only quiet place Esteban could find was the large private bathroom off Uncle Pedro's office. One door led to his office, the other to his bedroom, which was larger and more opulent than his office. The doors on either side could lock, a security precaution to satisfy Pedro's paranoia against night visitors bearing gifts. The large bathroom had a pedestal sink with gold faucets, a bidet, an American-styled toilet, and an immense porcelain bathtub adorned with gold hardware. His uncle had become a wealthy man who kept his real riches hidden from the outside world. Uncle Pedro could hide his secrets well, even from those close to him.

After much discussion about how this was to be done, Father Esteban found himself seated on a rail in the bathtub, with the bath curtain drawn around him. The young lady sat on the toilet lid. The arrangement gave the illusion of a booth, and the confession began.

"Forgive me, Father, for I have sinned. It's been six months since my last confession," the beautiful young woman said.

"What are your sins," Father Esteban asked.

And she began her confession. He was surprised and relieved because her confession was pretty much like the other confessions he'd experienced during the past year. *This will be easy,* he thought.

"I've been sleeping with an older man for six months. I'm feeling guilty and need absolution. That man is Pedro."

At first, Esteban didn't understand what she was talking about, but it sunk in. He was grateful for the curtain because he knew he wouldn't be able to hide his shock. She was talking about his Pedro. His Uncle Pedro! She continued to provide details of their relationship. "Father Esteban, help me cleanse my soul. What is my penance?"

Father Esteban didn't know what to say. After a few moments of silence, he asked, "What do you think your penance should be?"

This was the first time she'd been asked a question like this. She had to think about it, and after deliberating the question, she answered, "Three Rosaries and four thousand Euros in the poor box."

Four thousand Euros was a substantial amount of money, and all Father Esteban could say was, "Your penance is two Rosaries and one thousand Euros in the poor box. Go and sin no more."

The confession was over. The curtain was drawn back, and Esteban had to act like nothing was said. The confessional is sacred. Even Jesus, who had heard every word, acted as if the event had not occurred. They returned to the party.

A short time later, Esteban said to Jesus, "What did you think about that?"

"About what?"

"About the confession," said Esteban.

"You did a good job. You listened, you retained the sin, and you remitted the sin. That's what a priest does. All's good," Jesus said.

"But what about what she said about Uncle Pedro? What did you think about that?"

"It's not important. You should have forgotten about that already. Your job is not to remember. Your job is not to talk about it. You are my servant, my representative. You are to listen for me, to retain for me, and to remit for me. It is the act of forgiveness that counts. Nothing else. You are not to talk about her confession ever again. Your oath is to retain and remit. That is what is sacred. Do you think there's any more sausage and peppers?"

By one in the morning, Jesus complained he was dragging and feeling tired and wanted to go to bed. Esteban was also tired and wished to go to bed. Esteban announced he would be headed out. He thanked his mother for making such an incredible party, shook his Uncle Pedro's hand, and walked back to his cell at the seminary. It had been a long, long day, starting with his ordination and ending with a shocking confession he'd already forgotten.

His last words to Jesus as he said goodnight was, "I can't wait to hear about what I'll be doing in the Vatican."

Jesus' last words were spoken with a quiet chuckle. "Yes, tomorrow you'll get your first real assignment as a priest."

Jesus awoke from a deep, sound sleep by Father Esteban rattling around the room. "For pity's sake," he said, "what's all this ruckus? What time is it, anyway?"

"It's time to get up and for us to get going. It's already eight-thirty, and you've missed breakfast."

"Really?" Jesus said, moaning. "That's okay. I'm not feeling hungry."

"I'm not surprised after the way you ate last night. I'm surprised you didn't make yourself sick," Esteban said.

"I was." Jesus sighed. "A tad too much wine, me thinks."

"A tad too much of everything, me thinks," Esteban said smiling.

Jesus lay in his bed and watched Esteban pack his things and get dressed. Today Esteban wore a brand-new black suit, black shirt, black shoes with an uber-high shine, and the whitest of collars. All the new clothes were gifts from Uncle Pedro and his mother. Pride in Esteban ran deep and strong. Jesus bore all the rattling noise in quiet desperation. His head ached, and his sour stomach brought back the memories of the previous night's festivities.

"Why the new clothes, and why are you packing?" he asked.

"I'm a priest now, as you reminded me last night. I'll be

receiving my new assignment, so I'll want to look my best. I'm packing because I've graduated and can't live here any longer. They'll tell me where I'll live when they give me my assignment. Are you coming with me?"

"Do I have to?" Jesus asked.

"Not if you don't want to. It's up to you. It's your choice."

"Oh, well, since it's my choice. I'll see," Jesus answered. A few moments of silence elapsed. "Have you thought about what happens if you don't get that Vatican assignment?"

"No," Esteban said.

"Jesus, my head hurts," Jesus said.

"Serves you right for drinking that much," Esteban said. "I'm going to get the Vatican assignment. I was told by two classmates who overheard the conversations. They wouldn't lie. Priests don't ever lie."

"Good to know," Jesus said.

At 9:30 a.m., Esteban rolled up his mattress. He had finished packing and cleaning the room for one last time. The room was cleaner now than the day he moved in and more than ready for the next hopeful occupant. He was nothing if not clean and neat, a discipline hammered home to him from early childhood by his mother. After giving his cell one last visual inspection, he left and began his walk to the chapel.

As usual, Father Peter stood at the altar, but today there was a change in his manner. He looked friendly and happy. It looked like there might even be tears in his eyes. As the new priests filed in, he felt enthusiastic to see them and greeted them as equals. He referred to each person by his title and name. It was a glorious and happy day. When all were assembled, he led the newly ordained fathers in a prayer of thanksgiving. With no preamble, he began with a simple, "Let us pray," and the chapel fell silent as each new priest recognized for the first time the solemnity of the moment. Every new priest will say it's not the ordination that makes the realization of the priesthood a fact, but rather the first act of clergy and being treated as an equal by a priest who has been a teacher or a mentor.

Father Peter said, "Amen," and the new priests responded, "Amen," with the unity of one voice. All in harmony and all in tune. The chapel was awash with happy feelings and brotherhood. Could it be that today was the real ordination? Today, with their brothers, with those they had sweated with for four years of study and effort. The feeling of the calling and the power of the spirit was with them and part of them. These men were now their families, and their churches would be their homes. With a simple "Let us pray," this all became clear to everyone, including Father Esteban.

"Fathers, brothers," Father Peter said with a smile. "You will receive your assignments today. On the tables in the back are envelopes containing postings and instructions. On the front, we've marked a time and room number. It's imperative that you show up on time. You'll be receiving additional information regarding your new duties. This is the last time we'll be together like this. I am proud to say that I know you."

He raised his hands and said, "May our Lord Jesus Christ bless you and keep you. May he keep you in health, and may you find true happiness in his service all the days of your life, and in his name."

Everyone responded, "Amen."

With perfect good order, each priest went to the back of the chapel and found his paperwork. Much to his surprise,

Esteban saw his appointment was right then and there, and he was to head over to the Office of the Abbot.

"See," he said to Jesus. "I'm first, so it must be good." Jesus nodded.

Father Peter and the abbot were both standing in front of the abbot's desk when Father Esteban entered the office.

"Come in, come in," the abbot said. "May I get you some coffee?" Esteban was stunned. These high-ranking officials had never offered him anything.

"No, thank you, Father," Father Esteban answered.

"In that case, please take a seat and sit down," the abbot said. He pointed to a chair. "Have you read your assignment?"

"Not yet," Father Esteban said.

"Well, you'd better."

As Father Esteban opened the envelope, the abbot continued. "I'd like you to know the importance of this assignment. The awarding of this assignment was at the urging of the Pope himself. It fell to either you or Father Sergey. We selected you, Father Esteban, to be the personal representative of His Holiness."

While the abbot oozed charm and spoke glowingly of the assignment, Father Esteban read, with mounting horror, about where he had been posted and what his duties entailed. The abbot's voice was pushed to the background.

"It's not everyone who graduates and gets his own church out of the gate. Nevertheless, we share His Holiness' confidence that you'll be an outstanding representative for him. The Cardinal of Mexico will brief you upon your arrival next week. Do you have any questions?"

Father Esteban was flummoxed and speechless.

"No? Good. Good luck, and may God bless you." The

abbot took Father Esteban by the arm and led him to the door. "If anything should come up or you have any questions, call the administrator's office. They'll help you. Good day, Father."

"Oh, one more thing less I forget," the abbot said, "Weren't you born in Mexico? So, it'll be nice to spend some time back home!"

With that, Father Esteban found himself outside the abbot's office. Father Sergey was waiting for his turn. As the door closed behind him, Father Peter said to the abbot, "That was beautiful. I've never heard you make a lousy posting sound so impressive."

"We do our best," the abbot said waving away the compliment. "Let's get Father Sergey in here and get this over with."

Jesus caught up with a dazed Esteban within steps of walking away from the abbot's office. "Tell me, what happened?"

"I'm being shipped to Mexico."

"I know," Jesus said.

Reflecting on the assignment rumor, he surmised the intelligence had been flawed. He learned about Sergey's appointment during the next few days and was heartbroken.

"Why me?" he said to Jesus on the way to the airport.

"We all have to spend some time in the desert," Jesus replied.

"But Sergey is staying here. When will he be in the desert?" Esteban asked as they got on the plane for London, the first leg of the long trip.

"As of right now," Jesus said.

Then, he laughed.

CHAPTER 15

JETSETTER

Esteban and Jesus arrived early at the airport to be on the safe side. Esteban was anxious and nervous, thanks to his high-functioning condition. He'd been given little time to say goodbye as the seminary tended to move the new assignees out fast. To their credit, the Gregorian administration was efficient in getting done what needed to get done once it had the go-ahead. Inside Esteban's travel folder were his itinerary, tickets, and a credit card issued by the Vatican Bank. The itinerary included detailed instructions about the whats, wheres, and whens of the entire trip, including where to go upon his arrival in Mexico City. A separate sheet of paper included a list of email addresses, organized by city, of the clergy he could contact for additional help. No details appeared to have been overlooked or withheld. Esteban wasn't a test case!

Isabella gushed over his assignment and made it sound like he was a missionary sent out to save the souls of the wild. In other words, she made the new assignment sound like the

Church couldn't survive without her son. Her freshly minted Father Ferrari was going back to their roots, her roots. Jesus was bemused by the whole situation. Even with strangers, Isabella got carried away. First, she bragged about how important this assignment was and how he was going by special request of the His Holiness. Behind closed doors, she planned what she had to do next.

"Don't worry, my sister," Pedro said. "I'm sure he'll be able to cope. Esteban is a fine, strong, and independent young man. He's now a priest and heading off as a man of God. Jesus will be sure to look after him. If we don't see him again, we'll see him again in heaven. But I know you'll see him soon."

The ticket agent at the passenger check-in counter was courteous and respectful. She had boarded many newly ordained priests during the past two years and knew they weren't seasoned flyers. She reviewed the tickets and checked the Vatican-issued passport. Esteban's two bags were weighed and placed on the conveyor belt.

"Father, you'll need to reclaim your bags at Kennedy and again in Mexico City. You won't need to clear customs in London or Dallas, but you will in New York City and Mexico. You'll be kept in the passport control area between flights in London. Would you prefer window or aisle?"

"I'm thinking an aisle, please," Father Esteban answered.

"Good choice," Jesus said. He was also starting to exhibit signs of nerves connected to the travel.

"We'll put you in 2B, a very comfortable seat," the agent said. "We'll begin boarding in about four hours, and we'll be serving dinner on the flight. Father, there is no need to be nervous or to worry. All the other priests who have flown out from here have always come back to tell me how lovely everything was."

"Thank you for everything. May the Lord be with you," Esteban said. He revealed a smile of appreciation for the agent's kindness.

The flight left on time and flew into London's Heathrow airport, landing on the northern 27R runway. Unfortunately, the excellence of the onboard meal was short of the benchmark set by his mother. Jesus expressed his succinct thoughts as to the food quality, "Meh!" But didn't hesitate to get tucked in, nonetheless.

Esteban had the same seat on the connecting flight to JFK. The second leg of the trip felt like forever, and Esteban lost track of time. He had no watch, and his body was beginning to feel the effects of jet-lag. The flight arrived shortly after 1:00 a.m. He was tired, confused, and out of sorts. He cleared customs, which took almost an hour, and he had no issues collecting his checked luggage from the carousel. The check-in counters for his 6:00 a.m. flight to Dallas weren't going to open until 5:00 a.m. Not knowing what to do or where to go, he stood in line alone. The overhead monitors displayed a quarter to three.

As the clock struck five, the man behind the counter, a true New Yorker with a heavy Bronx accent, shouted, "Next." Esteban realized he'd nodded off while standing and had trouble understanding the man's his words.

"I'm flying to Mexico City and changing planes in Dallas," Esteban said.

The man took Esteban's tickets and said, "We've had a change of equipment for this flight. I'm going to have to give you a window seat in coach. This flight makes an additional stop in Saint Louis, so don't get off until you've reached Dallas." He handed back Esteban's reissued ticket. "Gate 42. Have a good trip, young man."

Esteban was not used to being spoken to so directly. Even Jesus was more polite to him, and Jesus was always teasing or nagging him about something. Esteban boarded a Boeing 737, and his seat was all the way toward the back. The seat had no real view of the outside. In addition, the seat was uncomfortable when compared to the previous ones. The flight attendants were polite and served hot coffee, orange juice, and a small breakfast sandwich. The flight took over three hours to reach Saint Louis. He attempted to strike up a conversation with the man sitting next to him but found it impossible. The plane was noisy. Hearing anything over the engine's drone was nigh on impossible. In addition, the man spoke with a flat, southern accent unique to Missouri's Ozark region. The accent didn't reverberate in a recognizable way inside Esteban's ear canal.

Upon the descent, Esteban couldn't believe the pain in his ears. The change in cabin air pressure made for an uncomfortable twelve minutes. He abided by the words of the ticket agent at JFK and stayed on board. The plane was refueled and reprovisioned. New passengers piled into the cabin. Esteban stewed in his seat, feeling even more tired and irritable. He was getting a headache and feeling sick to his stomach. An attendant noticed Esteban's drained coloring and convinced him to drink some iced water with a salt pill.

"Not too long to go, and you'll be able to get off and stretch your legs," she said in a kind tone and with a broad smile that showed off her whitened teeth.

At around 11:30 a.m., washed out, used up, and sizzled, he

stood before a Spanish-speaking ticket agent in Terminal D at the Dallas-Fort Worth Airport.

"*Buenos noches, Señor.* You have a ticket for this flight, *si?*"

The overtired young Father Ferrari presented his ticket and his credentials.

"*Gracias,*" the agent said and examined each document. "Everything is in order, Father. I'll make an announcement when it is time to board."

"May I ask how long it'll be before we leave?" Esteban had now been traveling for more than twenty-four hours.

"The boarding process will start in about two hours, and we're currently scheduled to depart at ten past two. And I'm seeing an arrival time shortly before five," the agent said looking down at his monitor.

Esteban figured he should be at the hotel and able to crash by seven. *That'll leave plenty of time to rest, get cleaned up, and be ready to meet the Cardinal in the morning at ten,* he thought.

"*Un momento, Padre,*" the agent said.

"*Si?*"

"Air traffic control has posted a delay for your Aeroméxico flight."

"Ugh."

The agent shrugged his shoulders and replied, "There's always a delay. Who can say why."

"Do you have any idea how long?"

"It's not for me to say. We'll leave when everything is ready."

Esteban didn't know what to ask next. He had a bad feeling and a premonition the trip was likely to get worse before it got better. Due to his fatigue, Esteban became agitated.

"What do you mean it's not for you to say? If it's not for you to say, who can say?" he asked.

"That's not for me to say."

Esteban was stuck. They had been conversing in Spanish, and the nuances of the language left for ambiguities. He was now certain he wasn't going to find out when the plane would leave.

Readjusting his attitude, Esteban asked the agent, "What do I have time to do while I wait?"

"What would you like to do?"

"That depends. What do I have time for?"

"That's not for me to say," the agent said.

Defeated, Esteban opted to change the line of questioning. "Where should I wait?"

"Wherever you'd like, Father."

"Is everyone going to be like this?" Esteban asked Jesus while thinking this agent was helping put some of Uncle Pedro's idiosyncrasies into context.

While winking, Jesus issued a large grin and said, "It's not for me to say."

By this time, a long line of passengers had formed behind Esteban. Most of the people appeared to be Mexican, and they all seemed accepting of the transactional slowness as a natural phenomenon. Each person waited in turn to hear the story of the delay and slumped back to wait on a chair or to sit on the floor. Disgruntled to the nth degree, Esteban found an unoccupied chair.

Jesus flopped next to him.

"I'm hot," Esteban said.

"Me too," Jesus said.

"I'm thirsty."

"Me too. Let's get ourselves something to drink."

The two amigos found a snack bar, and when Esteban asked what there was to drink, the woman behind the counter, in an ultra-slow and elongated southern drawl, replied, "Dac-tah Pearrr-pah, Co-Kaah Coe-lah, Awe-renge Cru-shh." Esteban wasn't familiar with these names and thought it might be her accentuated enunciation, so he asked her to repeat herself. So far, each of the Americans he'd spoken with sounded different, and nobody seemed to sound like his dad.

"Dac-tah Pearrr-pah or Co-Kaah Coe-lah or Awe-renge Cru-shh," she repeated with an uncharacteristic frown. *Dhese farners doen't unnerstan' en-e-thin'*, she thought.

Esteban thought he'd give the Dac-tah Pearrr-pah a try. He had no idea what he'd get, but he ordered it the same way the waitress spoke. The waitress turned away and came back with a bottle filled with a caramel-colored liquid. Esteban watched as she twisted the metal cap with her hand, releasing a quick hiss. The cap disappeared from view, and she poured the liquid into a large plastic cup filled with large cubes of ice. She placed the drink in front of Esteban on a paper coaster and said, "Here yew go, hun." The waitress diverted her undivided attention to a person standing next to Esteban and said loudly and slowly, "May I hep yew?"

Esteban walked over to the table where Jesus was sitting and carried his cup and coaster. The Dac-tah Pearrr-pah had multiple strange flavors, all intertwined and yet separate. It was sweet and tangy and cold. He drank it down and released a burp from the carbonation. Jesus' burp was far louder and quite insufferable.

Around 3:15 p.m., Esteban could still see the flight's passengers sitting, and nobody seemed upset. But Esteban was getting anxious, so he went and asked the agent if there was any news.

"About what?" the agent asked.

"About what time is the flight going to leave?" Esteban said finding himself getting angry all over again.

Despite his repeated requests for information, Esteban would receive a polite reply of, "It's not for me to say." Flustered, he returned to his Dac-tah Pearrr-pah, waiting on the table where it had been left.

At 9:00 p.m., he felt queasy, and a few minutes later, he rushed off to the men's room in short strides. It was a mild case of diarrhea caused by his fatigue rather than anything else. Mother Nature called several more times, but he was all good by 10:30 p.m. At eleven, a voice came over the Tannoy announcing the delayed 2:10 p.m. Aeroméxico flight to Mexico City would board in thirty-five minutes.

A middle-aged Mexican lady noticed Esteban was a priest, and the newfound knowledge the flight would soon leave stirred some primitive fear within her. She moseyed over to Father Ferrari in a gait Esteban would learn to recognize. He referred to it as the *Por Favor* Shuffle.

"*Por favor*, Father, will you please hear my confession before we leave?" the nice lady asked.

Father Esteban didn't know what to say, but Jesus coached him by reminding him that a priest's principal job was to hear confession. Esteban scanned the area and noticed a quiet corner that would suffice for an ad hoc situation.

"Of course," Father Ferrari said and led the way over to the corner. The lady's confession was a pleasant story, and she asked for the Lord's Prayer, which Esteban recited in Spanish. The lady recited the prayer with him, and he even found the ritual comforting in these less-than-ideal conditions. Father Ferrari dispensed a minimal penance based on her plea. They finished with a Hail Mary. Both stood and walked back to the gate and took their respective seats. Within moments, a line formed around Father Esteban. Many of the passengers scheduled for this flight were devout Catholics. At the end of each confession, Esteban would hear the word "Amen" followed by "*Gracias*" and feel one or two coins pressed into his hand. "*Por favor,* for the poor box," they would say.

By midnight, he was ready to board the plane for the final leg of his journey. But he and everyone else were still waiting to hear the official boarding announcement. He looked to the gate agent to make the announcement and didn't see him at the counter. Worried, he looked around and noticed the agent was walking out of the boarding area carrying a briefcase. Panic set in, and Esteban hurried over to the agent.

"When will we board?"

The agent gave him a smile, which Esteban was starting to dislike, and said, "It's not for me to say, *Señor.*"

"Are you leaving?"

"*Si, Padre.* It is time for me to go home."

"Well, who will tell us when to get on the plane?" Esteban asked.

"It's not for me to say," was the answer.

"You're leaving us here?"

"*Si, Señor.* It is time for me to go home. *Buenos noches,*" the agent said, and he departed.

As Esteban didn't know what else to do, he went to sit back down.

"I'm beginning to wonder if this flight will ever take off," he said to Jesus.

Jesus had taken off his black coat, loosened his collar, and adopted a relaxed and not-a-care-in-world-looking manner. He looked at Esteban through heavy-lidded eyes and said, "It's not for me to say, *Padre*."

At 1:00 a.m., a man wearing a pilot's uniform stepped into the boarding area and announced, "Everyone heading to Mexico City, please make your way down the jet bridge."

Those passengers who had not fallen asleep awakened those sleeping. Everyone gathered their belongings and waddled like a colony of penguins toward the boarding door. Through the gate area's large window, everyone noticed how the illuminated airplane's nose was attracting a gazillion moths, all dancing to the beat of their own drummers. Each passenger passed through the gate door, down the jet bridge, and into the plane. They pushed on through the narrow aisle to find and take their seat.

When Esteban got to his preassigned seat, he found it occupied, "*Por favor, Señor*," he said, "You are sitting in my seat. No?"

The man looked up with a blank expression. "*Por favor*," he replied. "Does it make a difference? Aren't we all going to the same place?"

Esteban was taken aback and found he had no answer, so he walked farther back into the plane and took an empty seat. Getting all the passengers seated took the better part of a half-hour. He looked around, taking stock of the airplane, and couldn't believe all the packages being brought on board. Over the next hour and a half, the plane didn't budge. The pilot and copilot would yoyo back and forth from the cockpit no less than five times. Each time one of them came out, they told everyone, "It won't be long now." No explanation was ever extended as to why the plane wasn't leaving. None of the passengers were able to detect any outside activity to attribute to the delay.

At 3:00 a.m., the engines roared to life, and the main boarding door was closed and locked. Without any fanfare, the plane was pushed back and began to taxi out to the runway. The pilot made an announcement about fastening seat belts, and the aircraft began lumbering down the runway. A second announcement followed, "Flight attendants, please take your seats." Within moments, the engines roared into life, Esteban felt his body being squeezed into his seat, and the front of the plane began to tilt upwards. They were in the air and heading away from DFW.

The plane picked up speed and altitude, banked to the southwest, and headed toward Mexico City. An attendant appeared from nowhere and offered soft drinks and precious little else. She seemed to be more frightened than the passengers. For four hours, the plane droned all the way to Mexico City. The frequency of the droning and the accompanying vibration made it next to impossible to settle down and sleep. Close to 6:00 a.m., the pilot came over the intercom system, "*Buenos días*. We hope everyone got some rest. Air traffic control has us in a holding pattern. We should be landing shortly."

The sun came up and threw unusual shadows all around the cabin. The morning rays helped to warm the chilled, ambient air. At 7:30 a.m. the plane landed and taxied to a stop in front of a small terminal. The plane boarding door opened, and the passengers lost no time gathering their belongings to disembark. It took Esteban another couple of hours to collect his two bags and clear customs.

Esteban entered the arrival hall and glanced over the instructions written on his itinerary. He saw that if his airplane landed more than thirty minutes after its scheduled landing time, he was to find a taxi for the short trip to the rectory. Although Esteban and Jesus had only been in the arrival hall for a few minutes, Jesus had managed to find the time to come by a woven straw sombrero with a wide brim. From looking around, the headwear style seemed to be popular. Esteban also noticed Jesus was now wearing his black coat draped over one shoulder and had ditched his shoes for sandals. His Roman collar was hanging from his shirt and was sweat-stained with grime.

"Ah, look, there's a sign for the taxis." Jesus pointed.

The time was approaching 10:00 a.m., and rush-hour traffic had not relented. The ride took an hour and forty minutes. As the taxi pulled in front of the rectory, the driver asked for four-hundred pesos. Father Esteban handed the driver his Vatican Bank credit card.

"*Padre, solo efectivo*, cash only," the driver said.

Esteban pulled out the coins collected from last night's airport confessional. These coins had been earmarked for the poor box; he grimaced at the thought. He placed each coin on the driver's open palm, one at a time, while counting aloud.

"Three hundred and eighty, three hundred and eighty-two, three hundred and eighty-seven, three hundred and eighty-eight, four hundred and eight."

"*Gracias, Padre, puedes dame un consejo*, can you give me a tip, *por favor?*"

Father Esteban only had a few more coins. So, without

bothering to count, he handed them all over. "*Gracias*," Esteban said.

He was now standing outside the taxi, by the curb, with two bags in his hand and facing the rectory. He was dog-tired beyond belief.

CHAPTER 16

THE CARDINAL OF MEXICO

He knocked at the rectory door. Nothing. He knocked again, louder. This time he was greeted by the housekeeper who received a heavy-duty whiff of this filthy traveling priest. The weary jet-setter had been on the road for several days. His appearance was unkempt, unshaven, and disheveled. And, he smelled dreadful.

"*Si*," the housekeeper said.

Esteban explained he had arrived from Rome on a long and tiring trip. He mentioned he was to arrive last night, but a serious flight delay prevented a timely arrival.

"Father Miguel Diego should be expecting me," said Esteban. "May I use your bathroom, *por favor*?"

"The Father has sat down for lunch. I'll let him know you've arrived. The bathroom door is down this hallway to the left," she said. Esteban put down his bags, and both headed off in separate directions.

When Esteban returned to the entryway and waited along with his bags. After about twenty minutes of standing, his mouth opened and took on a contorted shape as he exhaled a significant and loud yawn. Before he finished, Father Diego appeared. "Oh, dear. Excuse me, Father," Esteban said.

Esteban still looked a mess and still smelled too high heaven. "So, you're the new priest! Welcome. You were expected yesterday! Anyway, follow me. His Eminence is waiting for you."

Hearing what Father Diego said, a feather would have knocked Esteban over. *You can't be serious? You've got to be absolutely, one hundred thousand percent kidding me,* were the words that went through his head. "Marvelous" was the word that came out of his mouth.

Together, they walked at pace across the courtyard and entered the offices of the Mexican See. The priests and officials warmly acknowledged Father Diego as they made their way through the halls to the office of the cardinal.

"The cardinal is busy, but when I told him you'd arrived, he said he wanted to see you immediately," Father Diego told Esteban. Both fathers now stood outside the outer office housing the waiting area and administrative functions. The office was cool, airy, and well-lit.

At the entrance door to the cardinal's office was a secretary's desk occupied by a priest dressed in a clean, well-pressed white robe. He wore a black skull cap adorned with piping dyed in a rich red hue. A matching-colored red rope sash girded his waist. He had the appearance of a man of importance. Esteban noticed there were other priests in the office. They wore the same type of robe, but their black skull caps bore no piping, and their rope sashes were plain black. *Could it be they use colors to denote rank here?* He wondered. *Will I be given a blue sash?*

Father Diego and the priest behind the desk exchanged greetings, and Father Esteban was introduced to the others in the room. The introductions occurred so fast that Esteban never caught their names. In the long run, this didn't cause a problem; he never saw these men again.

"You may be seated over here," the priest behind the desk said. He pointed to a straight-backed chair. "His Eminence will be with you shortly." The priest also reacted as though he'd caught a whiff of something well past its sell-by date.

Esteban walked over to the chair and sat, and began to wait. He was tired, and the trip had not been without its stress, so he rested his eyes for a minute. With his eyes closed, he tried to stay alert to the various sounds traversing the room. But he slipped off into a comfortable slumber when the ring of a telephone brought him back to the present. He used his right hand to cover a muffled yawn and looked toward the desk clock. The time was seventeen minutes past three.

A constant stream of people kept coming in and out of the office. Had they forgotten about him? He continued to sit silently and motionless. Nobody asked if he was hungry or thirsty. Nobody offered food of any kind. Some of the priests, he could hear, were leaving for an afternoon break. Nobody seemed interested in offering him any sustenance. He hadn't eaten in a long time, and he hadn't had a drink for hours. His throat was parched. Even Jesus complained. Jesus must have sensed they would have to continue waiting because he decided to stretch out on the floor near Esteban's feet. From time to time, he would also yawn, stretch his arms out wide, and say, "The floor tile is hard, but at least it's pleasantly cool."

"We've been in here for more than three hours. Do you think they forgot about us?" Esteban asked Jesus.

"I don't know about you, but I know they've forgotten about me!" Jesus replied.

"What should I do?" Esteban asked.

"It's not for me to say." Jesus shrugged from the floor.

"Should I ask the priest sitting behind the desk?"

Jesus only shrugged again.

By late afternoon, Esteban was getting tired again. He was still thirsty and hungry and didn't want to wait any longer. He had made up his mind. "I'm going to say something to the priest," he told Jesus.

Esteban stood up and stepped over Jesus. With great purpose, he took a few steps and stood at the long edge of the desk. Before Esteban could utter a word, the priest looked up and said, "Ah, the Cardinal's ready to see you now."

He couldn't believe it. They had him wait for over five hours without offering him so much as a glass of water, and now the cardinal was ready. In a wave of nervousness, he realized he had to use the toilet.

"*Padre, lo siento,* I'm sorry. Would it be possible, by any chance, for me to use the bathroom before my visit?"

The priest's face remained impassive as he gave Esteban the go-ahead. Following the priest's directions, he hurried away and found relief and sanctuary. He used the facilities and washed his hands and face. Next, he took a long draught of cool water from the spigot. He sped back to the office to see the priest behind the desk.

"Ah, good," the priest behind the desk said. "We can go in." He stood up and led Father Esteban Ferrari to meet His Eminence, the Cardinal of the Mexican See.

In Rome, there were many cardinals. In the Vatican, where many more cardinals live and work, a cardinal's name might be substituted with his function or responsibility. Yet, in Mexico, there was only one cardinal. *Would this cardinal have a name?* Esteban wondered. Father Ferrari found himself standing before the cardinal. The one cardinal for an entire country.

The office was whoppingly spacious with high ceilings. Suspended from the ceiling were four large fans that turned slowly to prevent the air from stagnating. Like the ante office, the room was well-lit with light emanating from long expansive windows. The walls were papered with light pastel-colored fabrics so as not to distract from the paintings none of which would have been out of place in any of the world's great art galleries. There was a Titian, a Picasso, a Renoir, a Van Gogh, a Caravaggio, a Mango, and a Raphael. Between each painting was a sculpted figure or bust. All these works of art were displayed for the cardinal's personal pleasure. The room was air-conditioned with equipment mounted in two high windows and covered and silenced so as not to intrude. In addition, the floors were terracotta with bright glazed tones. Together, all these things made the room inviting despite its outrageous size.

The cardinal was seated on a cushioned, gilded chair situated on a riser three steps above the floor in the center of the room. The chair had a high back. Under the cardinal's feet was a small, padded footstool. Draped around the chair was red satin bunting, which covered the floor and sides of the dais. The three steps were covered with white satin, and the top step was padded so visitors could kiss the cardinal's ring without hurting their knees. Context is essential, for the cardinal's chair could have been mistaken for a throne in a different setting.

The cardinal was dressed in a pale red robe made from

patterned silk. The robe had a large flounce collar covering the shoulders. The collar was of a lighter shade of red, closer to pink. The collar was embroidered with dark red crosses entwined with a gold thread. The collar, hem, and sleeves were trimmed with a strip of piped white fur. An embroidered miter constructed of silk, linen, and leather was upon his head. On his feet were slippers of the same color as his miter.

Next to the cardinal's chair was a small table. On the desk was a gold cup from which the cardinal would sip iced coffee or iced chocolate. There was also a gold plate with fresh fruit. The cardinal had several robe-dressed priests bustling about him, carrying out his slightest order or request. As the priests left the cardinal to carry out a task, they went to one of the many desks behind the cardinal's back. The Vatican offices held no superiority over the majesty of this office. Esteban was in awe and frozen in his place before this all-powerful man. After several minutes, the cardinal looked down at young Esteban and motioned him forward. Father Ferrari stepped up and kissed the ring and, misjudging the steps, stumbled backward.

"So, you're the priest our Pope sent me to fill my long-empty vacancy," the cardinal said, wearing what Esteban mistook for a smile.

Before Esteban could muster the beginnings of a response, the cardinal continued. "You are the priest that comes before me in soiled clothing and in a desperate state of needing a bath? You are the priest that keeps a cardinal waiting while you go to the bathroom? This is the kind of priest the Holy Father chooses to send me? Are you not a graduate of the Gregorian seminary who is supposed to be so brilliant? Are you not the priest the Holy Father sent me to curry my favor in hopes of winning my support? I think not. You're a boy in priest's clothing. My request to His Holiness was for a real priest to get Las Cruces contributing again," the Cardinal said. His voice was raised. It sounded like thunder.

Father Ferrari stood there, dazed and confused. *What is the cardinal talking about?* he wondered. He'd been sent to take over a church, and the cardinal was talking about contributions. Esteban had been told he was awarded this position, and the cardinal spoke about currying favor and winning support. What did this all mean? *What's going on?* wondered Esteban. The cardinal continued, "The Pope knows I did not vote for him, and I do not ascribe to all his decisions. Is this all some type of joke His Holiness has chosen to play? Could this be some type of payback on his part? Father Ferrari, I don't believe you can do what needs to be done at our church. To be frank, the local people have fallen away and have not had a priest for years. Las Cruces needs to be refurbished, and the people must begin to donate and contribute again. Do you believe you can prove me wrong? Can you, Father Ferrari, accomplish these things?"

Esteban was intimidated and tongue-tied, unable to utter a word. He was bewildered.

Jesus butted in, "*Amigo*," he said. "We must hurry and get to the desert. You're learning the truth. Just say, '*Si.*'"

"*Si*," Father Esteban Ferrari answered.

"*Muy bueno*, very good. I hope that is the case," the cardinal said. "Father Diego will give you further directions and see you on your way." Esteban stepped forward to kiss the cardinal's ring once again, and Father Diego led him away from the office.

Jesus laughed as he said to Esteban, "You know, my young

whippersnapper, you've flown across the Atlantic, traveled across multiple time zones, spent more than two days inside airplanes and airports, waited over five hours to meet the cardinal, and all you had to say for yourself was '*Sí.*' Way to go, *amigo. Muy bonito,* very nice. Very impressive."

"Ugh!" Esteban responded.

"Let's just chalk that one up to tough love," Jesus said.

The End

Follow Esteban on his journey to Las Cruces and beyond in Book Two—Esteban: Love's Irony.

ABOUT THE AUTHOR

FISH NEALMAN, a distinguished luminary in data-driven business decisions, is renowned for his insightful expertise, shared through a series of technical books. With a global footprint spanning numerous countries, his profound insights enrich his debut fictional trilogy, seamlessly blending imagination and reality. As a seasoned professional, he has collaborated with organizations worldwide, unlocking the untapped potential of data. Through his masterful storytelling, readers are transported to captivating realms, as his keen observations form the cornerstone of his transcendent tale.